Judy Moody

Books by Megan McDonald and Peter H. Reynolds:

#1 – *Judy Moody*
#2 – *Judy Moody Gets Famous!*
#3 – *Judy Moody Saves the World!*
#4 – *Judy Moody Predicts the Future*
#5 – *Judy Moody, M.D.: The Doctor Is In!*
#6 – *Judy Moody Declares Independence*
#7 – *Judy Moody Around the World in 8½ Days*
#1 – *Stink: The Incredible Shrinking Kid*
#2 – *Stink and the Incredible Super-Galactic Jawbreaker*
#3 – *Stink and the World's Worst Super-Stinky Sneakers*
The Judy Moody Mood Journal
Judy Moody's Double-Rare Way-Not-Boring Book of Fun Stuff to Do

Books by Megan McDonald:
Ant and Honey Bee: What a Pair!
The Sisters Club

Books by Peter H. Reynolds:
The Dot
Ish
So Few of Me

Judy Moody

Megan McDonald

illustrated by
Peter H. Reynolds

CANDLEWICK PRESS
CAMBRIDGE, MASSACHUSETTS

The author extends special thanks
to Hailey and Randi Reel.

Text copyright © 2000 by Megan McDonald
Illustrations copyright © 2000 by Peter H. Reynolds
Judy Moody font copyright © 2004 by Peter H. Reynolds

Judy Moody®. Judy Moody is a registered trademark
of Candlewick Press, Inc.

All rights reserved. No part of this book may be reproduced,
transmitted, or stored in an information retrieval system in any form
or by any means, graphic, electronic, or mechanical, including
photocopying, taping, and recording, without prior written
permission from the publisher.

First paperback edition in this format 2006

The Library of Congress has cataloged the hardcover edition as follows:
McDonald, Megan.
Judy Moody / Megan McDonald ; illustrated by Peter H. Reynolds. —
1st ed.
p. cm.
Summary: Third grader Judy Moody is in a first day of school bad
mood until she gets an assignment to create a collage all about
herself and begins creating her masterpiece, the Me collage.
ISBN 978-0-7636-0685-5 (hardcover)
[1. First day of school—Fiction. 2. Schools—Fiction.
3. Emotions—Fiction.]   I. Reynolds, Peter H., ill. II. Title.
PZ7.M478419Ju 2000
[Fic]—dc21   99-13464
ISBN 978-0-7636-1231-3 (paperback)

10

Printed in the United States of America

This book was typeset in Stone Informal.
The illustrations were done in watercolor, tea, and ink.

Candlewick Press
2067 Massachusetts Avenue
Cambridge, Massachusetts 02140

visit us at www.candlewick.com

For my sisters, Susan, Deborah, Michele, Melissa
M. M.

For my daughter, Sarah, and her cat, Twinkles
P. H. R.

Table of Contents

A Bad Mood...1

Roar!...11

Two Heads Are Better Than One...24

My Favorite Pet...40

My Smelly Pet...53

Doctor Judy Moody...60

The T.P. Club...72

Mouse

The Worst Thing Ever...86

Definitely the Worst Thing Ever...104

Rocky

The Funniest Thing Ever...111

Frank

The Me Collage...128

Band-Aids and Ice Cream...141

Mr. Todd

A Bad Mood

Judy Moody did not want to give up summer. She did not feel like brushing her hair every day. She did not feel like memorizing spelling words. And she did not want to sit next to Frank Pearl, who ate paste, in class.

Judy Moody was in a mood.

Not a good mood. A bad mood. A mad-face mood. Even the smell of her new Grouchy pencils could not get her out of bed.

"First day of school!" sang her mother. "Shake a leg and get dressed."

Judy Moody slunk down under the covers and put a pillow over her head.

"Judy? Did you hear me?"

"ROAR!" said Judy.

She would have to get used to a new desk and a new classroom. Her new desk would not have an armadillo sticker with her name on it, like her old one last year. Her new classroom would not have a porcupine named Roger.

And with her luck, she'd get stuck sitting in the first row, where Mr. Todd could see every time she tried to pass a note to her best friend, Rocky.

Mom poked her head inside Judy's room

again. "And think about brushing that hair, okay?"

One of the worst things about the first day of school was that everybody came back from summer wearing new T-shirts that said DISNEY WORLD or SEA WORLD or JAMESTOWN: Home of Pocahontas. Judy searched her top drawer and her bottom drawer and even her underwear drawer. She could not find one shirt with words.

She wore her tiger-striped pajama pants on the bottom and a plain old no-words T-shirt on top.

"She's wearing pajamas!" said her brother, Stink, when she came downstairs. "You can't wear pajamas to school!"

Stink thought he knew everything now that he was starting second grade. Judy glared at him with one of her famous troll-eyes stares.

"Judy can change after breakfast," Mom said.

"I made sunny-side-up eggs for the first day of school," said Dad. "There's squishy bread for dipping."

There was nothing sunny about Judy's egg—the yellow middle was broken. Judy slid her wobbly egg into the napkin on her lap, and fed it to Mouse, their cat, under the table.

"Summer is over, and I didn't even go anywhere," said Judy.

"You went to Gramma Lou's," said Mom.

"But that was right here in boring old Virginia. And I didn't get to eat hot dogs and ride a roller coaster or see a whale," said Judy.

"You rode a bumper car," said Mom.

"Baby cars. At the mall," Judy said.

"You went fishing and ate shark," said Dad.

"She ate a shark?" asked Stink.

"I ate a shark?" asked Judy.

"Yes," said Dad. "Remember the fish we bought at the market when we couldn't catch any?"

"I ate a shark!" said Judy Moody.

Judy Moody ran back to her room and peeled off her shirt. She took out a fat marker and drew a big-mouthed shark with lots of teeth. I ATE A SHARK, she wrote in all capitals.

Judy ran out the door to the bus. She didn't wait for Stink. She didn't wait for kisses from Dad or hugs from Mom. She was in a hurry to show Rocky her new T-shirt with words.

She almost forgot her bad mood until she saw Rocky practicing card tricks at the bus stop. He was wearing a giant-sized blue and white T-shirt with fancy letters and a picture of the Loch Ness Monster roller coaster.

"Like my new T-shirt?" he asked. "I got it at Busch Gardens."

"No," said Judy Moody, even though she secretly liked the shirt.

"I like your shark," said Rocky. When Judy didn't say anything, he asked, "Are you in a bad mood or something?"

"Or something," said Judy Moody.

Roar!

When Judy Moody arrived in third grade, her teacher, Mr. Todd, stood by the door, welcoming everyone. "Hello there, Judy."

"Hello, Mr. Toad," said Judy. She cracked herself up.

"Class, please hang your backpacks on the hooks and put your lunches in the cubbies," said Mr. Todd.

Judy Moody looked around the classroom.

"Do you have a porcupine named Roger?" Judy asked Mr. Todd.

"No, but we have a turtle named Tucson. Do you like turtles?"

She liked turtles! But she caught herself just in time. "No. I like toads." Judy cracked up again.

"Rocky, your seat is over by the window, and Judy, yours is right up front," said Mr. Todd.

"I knew it," said Judy. She surveyed her new front-row desk. It didn't have an armadillo sticker with her name on it.

Guess Who sat across the aisle from her. Frank Eats-Paste Pearl. He glanced at Judy sideways, then bent his thumb all the way back, touching his wrist. Judy

rolled her tongue like a hot dog back at him.

"You like sharks too?" he asked, passing her a small white envelope with her name on it.

Ever since they had danced the Maypole together in kindergarten, this boy would not leave her alone. In first grade, Frank Pearl sent her five valentines. In second grade, he gave her a cupcake on Halloween, on Thanksgiving, and on Martin Luther King Jr. Day. Now, on the first day of third grade, he gave her a birthday party invitation. Judy checked the date inside — his birthday was not for three weeks! Even a real shark would not scare him off.

"Can I look inside your desk?" asked Judy. He moved to one side. No sign of paste.

Mr. Todd stood in front of the class. GINO'S EXTRA-CHEESE PIZZA was printed in large letters on the board.

"Are we having extra-cheese pizza for lunch?" Judy asked.

"For Spelling." Mr. Todd held his finger to his lips like it was a secret. "You'll see."

Then he said, "Okay! Third grade! Listen up! We're going to try something different to kick off the year, as a way of getting to know one another. This year, each of you will make your own Me collage. All about YOU. You can draw or cut out pictures and paste things to your collage that tell the class what makes you YOU."

A Me collage! It sounded fun to Judy, but she didn't say so.

"We don't have to draw a map of our family, then?" asked Jessica Finch.

"I'm passing out a list of ideas for things you might include, like your family. I'm also giving everyone a folder for collecting the things you want to put on your collage. We'll work on these as we have time over the next month. At the end of September, you'll each get a chance to tell the class about YOU."

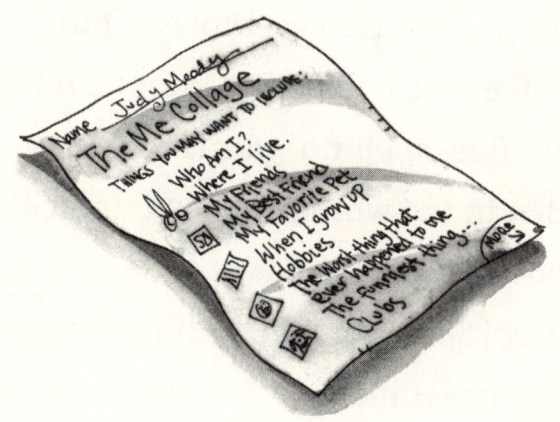

All through Language Arts and Social Studies, Judy thought about one thing—herself. Judy Moody, star of her own Me collage. Maybe third grade wasn't so bad after all.

"Okay, everybody. Time for Spelling."

"Yuck. Spelling," Judy said under her breath, remembering her bad mood.

"Yuck. Spelling," Frank Pearl agreed. Judy squinched her eyebrows at him.

"Take out a piece of paper and write down five spelling words you can find hidden in the words on the board, GINO'S EXTRA-CHEESE PIZZA."

"Cool Spelling, huh?" said a note passed to Judy by Frank.

"No," she wrote back on her hand, flashing it at him.

Judy took out her brand-new package of Grouchy pencils with mad faces on them. GROUCHY pencils—*for completely impossible moods,* said the package. *Ever see a pencil that looks like it got up on the wrong side of the bed?*

Perfect. The new Grouchy pencil helped her think. She found the words TREE, TEXAS, and TAXI hidden in Mr. Todd's spelling on the board. But instead she wrote down 1)NO 2)NO 3)NO 4)NO 5)NO.

"Who would like to tell the class five words they came up with?" asked Mr. Todd.

Judy's hand shot up.

"Judy?"

"NO, NO, NO, NO, NO!" said Judy.

"That's one word. I need four more. Come up and write them on the board."

Judy Moody did not write TREE,

TEXAS, and TAXI. Instead she wrote RAT and GNAT.

"How about BRAT?" called Rocky.

"There's no *B*," said Frank Pearl.

TIGER, wrote Judy.

"One more word," said Mr. Todd.

SPIT, wrote Judy.

"Can you use any of those words in a sentence, Judy?" asked Mr. Todd.

"The tiger spit on the rat and the gnat."

The whole class cracked up. Frank laughed so hard he snorted.

"Are you in a bad mood today?" asked Mr. Todd.

"ROAR," said Judy Moody.

"That's too bad," said Mr. Todd. "I was just about to ask who wants to go down to the office and pick up the pizza. It's a welcome-back surprise."

"Pizza? Pizza! For real?" The room buzzed with excitement.

Judy Moody wanted to be the one to pick up the pizza. She wanted to be the one to open the box. She wanted to be the one who got to keep the little three-legged plastic table that kept the box top from sticking to the pizza.

"So. Who would like to pick up the pizza today?" asked Mr. Todd.

"Me!" yelled Judy. "Me! Me! Me! Me! Me!" everyone shouted at once, waving their hands like windmills in the air.

Rocky raised his hand without saying a word.

"Rocky, would you like to pick up the pizza?"

"Sure!" said Rocky.

"Luck-y!" Judy said.

When Rocky came back with the pizza, the class grew quiet, everyone chewing teeny-weeny cheesy squares of Gino's pizza and listening to Mr. Todd read them a chapter from a book about a pepperoni pizza–eating dog.

When he finished reading, Judy asked, "Mr. Todd, can I look at your little pizza table?"

"That does look like a miniature table, Judy. I never thought of it that way."

"I collect them," said Judy Moody. She didn't really collect them—yet. So far, she had collections of twenty-seven dead moths, a handful of old scabs, a dozen fancy toothpicks, hundreds of designer Band-Aids (she needed the box tops), a box of body parts (from dolls!) including three Barbie heads, and four unused erasers shaped like baseballs.

"Tell you what," said Mr. Todd. "If you think you can come to third grade in a good mood tomorrow, it's yours. Do you think you can agree to that?"

"Yes, Mr. Todd," said Judy. "Yes, yes, yes, yes, YES!"

pizza table ↑

Two Heads Are Better Than One

Judy was teaching Mouse to walk on two legs when the phone rang.

"Hello?"

All she heard was air.

"Hello?" Judy asked the air.

"Hello, Judy? Are you allowed to come to my party?" a voice asked. A Frank Pearl voice. It had only been two days since he gave her the invitation.

"Wrong number," said Judy, hanging up. She dangled her new pizza table from a string in front of Mouse's nose.

The phone rang again. "Hello? Is this the Moodys'?"

"Not now, Frank. I'm in the middle of an important experiment."

"Okay. Bye."

The phone rang a third time.

"The experiment's not over yet," Judy yelled into the phone.

"What experiment?" asked Rocky.

"Never mind," said Judy.

"Let's go to Vic's," said Rocky. "I want to get something for my Me collage." Vic's was the Mini Mart down the hill where they had cool prizes in the jawbreaker machine, like tattoos that wash off and magic tricks.

"Let me ask," said Judy.

"Mom, can I go to Vic's with Rocky?"

"Sure," said Mom.

"Sure!" said Judy, tossing Mouse the pizza table.

"I'm going too," said Stink.

"No, you're not," Judy told him.

"You and Rocky can take him along," said Mom, giving her one of those looks.

"But he doesn't know about crossing through China and Japan on the way," Judy said. Only best friends knew that the first speed bump on the way was crossing into China, the second, Japan.

"I'm sure you could teach him," Mom said.

"Teach me," said Stink.

"Meet me at the manhole," Judy said back into the phone. The manhole was exactly halfway between Judy's front door and Rocky's. Over the summer they had measured it with a very long ball of string.

She ran out the door. Stink ran out the door after her.

Rocky had a dollar. Judy had a dollar. Stink had six pennies.

"If we put our money together, we can buy eight jawbreakers," said Rocky.

"Two heads are better than one," Judy laughed. "Get it?" She unscrunched the dollar bill from her pocket and pointed to George Washington's head.

"I've got six heads," said Stink, showing his pennies.

"That's because you're a monster! Get it?" Judy and Rocky cracked up.

Stink did not have enough money for even one jawbreaker. "You'll break your mouth if you try to eat eight jawbreakers," said Stink. "I could eat at least two for you."

"It's for the prizes," Judy told him.

"Eight quarters give us eight chances to win a magic trick," said Rocky. "I need a new magic trick to paste on my Me collage."

"Hey, wait!" said Judy. "I just remembered—I need my dollar to buy Band-Aids."

"Band-Aids are boring," said Stink. "Besides, you have ten million. Dad says we have more Band-Aids in our bathroom than the Red Cross."

"But I want to be a doctor," said Judy. "Like Elizabeth Blackwell, First Woman Doctor! She started her own hospital. She knew how to operate and put together body parts and everything."

"Body parts. Yuck!" Stink said.

"You saved Band-Aid box tops all summer," said Rocky. "I thought you had enough to send away for that doctor doll."

"I did. I already ordered it. Back in July. I'm still waiting for it to come. But now I need a microscope. You can look at blood or scabs or anything with it!"

Stink asked, "When do we get to China?"

"We're still on Jefferson Street, Stink," Rocky told him.

"Let's look for rocks until we get to China," said Stink.

"Let's see who can find the best one," said Rocky.

The three of them studied the ground as they walked. Judy found five pink pebbles and a Bazooka Joe comic with a fortune

5 pink pebbles   bubblegum fortune   blue lego   Lucky stone

that read: MONEY IS COMING YOUR WAY. Rocky found a blue Lego and a stone with a hole in the middle — a lucky stone!

"I found a black diamond!" said Stink.

"That's just charcoal," said Judy.

"It's just glass," Rocky said.

"Wait!" Judy said, crossing her eyes at Rocky. "I think it's a moon rock! Don't you, Rocky?"

"Yes," said Rocky. "Definitely."

"How do you know?" asked Stink.

"It has craters," Judy said.

"How did it get here?" asked Stink.

"It fell from the sky," said Judy.

"Really?" asked Stink.

"Really," said Rocky.

"In my *Space Junk* magazine, it tells how a moon rock fell from space and left a hole in Arizona once."

"And our teacher last year told us how a moon rock hit a dog in Egypt one time. No lie," Judy told her brother. "You're lucky. Moon rocks are billions of years old."

"*Space Junk* says moon rocks are dusty on the outside and sparkly on the inside," said Rocky.

"There's only one way to find out for sure if this is a moon rock then," said Judy. Judy scouted around for a large rock. Then she clobbered Stink's lump, smashing the moon rock to bits.

"You smashed it!" said Stink.

"Look, I think I see a sparkle!" said Rocky.

"Stink, you found a real moon rock, all right," Judy said.

"It's not a moon rock anymore!" cried Stink.

"Look at it this way, Stink," said Judy. "Now you have something better than a moon rock."

"What could be better than a moon rock?" asked Stink.

"Lots and lots of moon dust." Judy and Rocky fell down laughing.

"I'm going home," said Stink. He scraped up handfuls of the smashed rock, filling his pockets with dirt.

Judy and Rocky laughed the rest of the way to China, ran backward to Japan, then hopped on one foot while patting their heads until they got to Vic's.

At Vic's, they put their George Washington heads together for one small box of Band-Aids, and had enough left over for one jawbreaker each. Neither of them won a magic trick for Rocky's Me collage. Not even a troll or a miniature comic book or a tattoo.

"Maybe I could put a jawbreaker on my

collage," said Rocky. "Are you going to stick some Band-Aids on yours?"

"Hey, good idea," said Judy.

"Still a nickel left," Rocky said. So they bought a gumball and saved it for Stink.

When they reached Judy's driveway, Stink ran toward them, his pockets jangling with money. Stink had brown lunch bags lined up on the front steps.

"Guess what!" called Stink. "I made three dollars! Just since I got home."

"No way," said Judy.

"Let's see," said Rocky.

Stink emptied his pockets. Rocky counted twelve quarters.

"What's in the bags?" asked Judy.

"Everybody in the state of Virginia must want it."

"Yeah, what are you selling, anyway?" asked Rocky.

"Moon dust," said Stink.

My Favorite Pet

It was Labor Day, a no-school day. Judy looked up from her Me collage on the dining-room table.

"We need a new pet," Judy announced to her family.

"A new pet? What's wrong with Mouse?" asked Mom. Mouse opened one eye.

"I have to pick MY FAVORITE PET. How can I pick my favorite when I only have one?"

"Pick Mouse," said Mom.

"Mouse is so old, and she's afraid of everything. Mouse is a lump that purrs."

"You're NOT thinking of a dog, I hope," said Dad. Mouse jumped off the chair and stretched.

"Mouse would definitely not like that," said Judy.

"How about a goldfish?" asked Stink. Mouse rubbed up against Judy's leg.

"Mouse would like that too much," Judy said. "I was thinking of a two-toed sloth."

"Right," said Stink.

"They're neat," said Judy. She showed Stink its picture in her rain forest magazine. "See? They hang upside down all day.

They even sleep upside down."

"You're upside down," said Stink.

"What do they eat?" asked Dad.

"It says here they eat leaf-cutter ants and fire-bellied toads," Judy read.

"That should be easy," said Stink.

"Tell you what, Judy," said Dad. "Let's take a ride over to the pet store. I'm not saying we'll get a sloth, but it's always fun to look around. Maybe it'll even help me think of a five-letter word for fish that starts with *M* for my crossword puzzle."

"Let's all go," said Mom.

When they arrived at Fur & Fangs, Judy saw snakes and parrots, hermit crabs and guppies. She even saw a five-letter fish word beginning with *M*—a black molly.

"Do you have any two-toed sloths?" she asked the pet store lady.

"Sorry. Fresh out," said the lady.

"How about a newt or a turtle?" asked Dad.

"Did you see the hamsters?" asked Mom.

"Never mind," said Judy. "There's nothing from the rain forest here."

"Maybe they have a stinkbug," Stink said.

"One's enough," said Judy, narrowing her eyes at Stink.

They picked out a squeaky toy mouse for Mouse. When they went to pay for it, Judy noticed a green plant with teeth sitting on the counter. "What's that?" she asked the pet store lady.

"A Venus flytrap," the lady said. "It's not

an animal, but it doesn't cost much, and it's easy to take care of. See these things that look like mouths with teeth? Each one closes like a trap door. It eats bugs around the house. Like flies and ants, that sort of thing. You can feed it a little raw hamburger too."

"Rare," said Judy Moody.

"Cool," said Stink.

"Good idea," said Mom.

"Sold," said Dad.

Judy set her new pet on her desk, where the angle of sunlight hit it just right. Mouse watched from the bottom bunk, with one eye open.

"I can't wait to take my new pet to school

tomorrow for Share and Tell," Judy told Stink. "It's just like a rare plant from the rain forest."

"It is?" Stink asked.

"Sure," said Judy. "Just think. There could be a medicine hiding right here in these funny green teeth. When I'm a doctor,

I'm going to study plants like this and discover cures for ucky diseases."

"What are you going to name it?" asked Stink.

"I don't know yet," said Judy.

"You could call it Bughead, since it likes bugs."

"Nah," said Judy.

Judy watered her new pet. She sprinkled Gro-Fast on the soil. When Stink left, she sang songs to it. "I know an old lady who swallowed a fly. . . ." She sang till the old lady swallowed a horse.

She still couldn't think of a good name. Rumpelstiltskin? Too long. Thing? Maybe.

"Stink!" she called. "Go get me a fly."

"How am I going to catch a fly?" asked Stink.

"One fly. I'll give you a dime." Stink ran down to the window behind the couch and brought back a fly.

"Gross! That fly is dead."

"It was going to be dead in a minute anyway."

Judy scooped up the dead fly with the tip of her ruler and dropped it into one of the mouths. In a flash, the trap closed around the fly. Just like the pet store lady said.

"Rare!" said Judy.

"Snap! Trap!" Stink said, adding sound effects.

"Go get me an ant. A live one this time."

Stink wanted to see the Venus flytrap eat again, so he got his sister an ant. "Snap! Trap!" said Judy and Stink when another trap closed.

"Double rare," Judy said.

"Stink, go catch me a spider or something."

"I'm tired of catching bugs," said Stink.

"Then go ask Mom or Dad if we have any raw hamburger."

Stink frowned.

"Please, pretty please with bubble-gum ice cream on top?" Judy begged. Stink didn't budge. "I'll let you feed it this time."

Stink ran to the kitchen and came back with a hunk of raw hamburger. He plopped a big glob of hamburger into an open trap.

"That's way too much!" Judy yelled, but it was too late. The mouth snap-trapped around it, hamburger oozing out of its teeth. In a blink, the whole arm drooped, collapsing in the dirt.

"You killed it! You're in trouble, Stink. MOM! DAD!" Judy called.

Judy showed her parents what happened. "Stink killed my Venus flytrap!"

"I didn't mean to," said Stink. "The trap closed really fast!"

"It's not dead. It's digesting," said Dad. "The jaws will probably open by tomorrow morning," said Mom.

"Maybe it's just sleeping or something," said Stink.

"Or something," said Judy.

My Smelly Pet

Tomorrow morning came. The jaws were still closed. Judy tried teasing it with a brand new ant. "Here you go," she said in her best squeaky baby voice. "You like ants, don't you?" The jaws did not open one tiny centimeter. The plant did not move one trigger hair.

Judy gave up. She carefully lodged the plant in the bottom of her backpack. She'd take it to school, stinky, smelly glob of hamburger and all.

On the bus, Judy showed Rocky her new pet. "I couldn't wait to show everybody how it eats. Now it won't even move. And it smells."

"Open Sesame!" said Rocky, trying some magic words. Nothing happened.

"Maybe," said Rocky, "the bus will bounce it open."

"Maybe," said Judy. But even the bouncing of the bus did not make her new pet open up.

"If this thing dies, I'm stuck with Mouse for MY FAVORITE PET," Judy said.

Mr. Todd said first thing, "Okay, class, take out your Me collage folders. I'll pass around old magazines, and you can spend the next half-hour cutting out pictures for your collages. You still have over three weeks, but I'd like to see how everybody's doing."

Her Me collage folder! Judy had been so busy with her new pet, she had forgotten to bring her folder to school.

Judy Moody sneaked a peek at Frank Pearl's folder. He had cut out pictures of macaroni (favorite food?), ants (favorite pet?), and shoes. Shoes? Frank Pearl's best friend was a pair of shoes?

Judy looked down at the open backpack under her desk. The jaws were still closed. Now her whole backpack was smelly. Judy took the straw from her juice box and poked at the Venus flytrap. No luck. It would never open in time for Share and Tell!

"Well?" Frank asked.

"Well, what?"

"Are you going to come?"

"Where?"

"My birthday party. A week from Saturday. All the boys from our class are coming. And Adrian and Sandy from next door."

Judy Moody did not care if the president himself was coming. She sniffed her backpack. It stunk like a skunk!

"What's in your backpack?" Frank asked.

"None of your beeswax," Judy said.

"It smells like dead tuna fish!" Frank

Pearl said. Judy hoped her Venus flytrap would come back to life and bite Frank Pearl before he ever had another birthday.

Mr. Todd came over. "Judy, you haven't cut out any pictures. Do you have your folder?"

"I did—I mean—it was—then—well—no," said Judy. "I got a new pet last night."

"Don't tell me," said Mr. Todd. "Your new pet ate your Me collage folder."

"Not exactly. But it did eat one dead fly and one live ant. And then a big glob of . . ."

"Next time try to remember to bring your folder to school, Judy. And please, everyone, keep homework away from animals!"

"My new pet's not an animal, Mr. Todd," Judy said. "And it doesn't eat homework. Just bugs and raw hamburger." She pulled the Venus flytrap from her backpack. Judy could not believe her eyes! Its arm was no longer droopy. The stuck trap was now wide open, and her plant was looking hungry.

"It's MY FAVORITE PET," said Judy. "Meet Jaws!"

Doctor Judy Moody

Finally! Judy thought the only thing finer in the world than getting Jaws had to be getting a big brown box in the mail with the name DOCTOR Judy Moody on it. She was in an operating mood.

"Can I open it?" asked Stink, coming out of his closet fort.

"What does it say right there?" asked Judy, pointing to the label.

"Doctor Judy Moody," read Stink.

"Exactly," said Judy Moody. "I collected all the box tops."

"I got you some from the school nurse!" said Stink.

"Okay. You can go get the scissors."

Stink handed over the scissors. Judy poked through the tape and broke open the brown flaps. Mouse pawed at the sticky tape. Stink's head kept getting in the way.

"Stink! I'm in the middle of an operation!" Judy pulled aside the tissue paper and lifted out the doctor doll.

At last! Judy held the doll in her lap and stroked her silky smooth hair. She made neat little bows in the ties of the doll's blue and white hospital gown. The doll was wearing a hospital bracelet.

"Her name is Hedda-Get-Betta," Judy read.

"Does she do anything?" asked Stink.

"It says here if you turn the knob on top of her head, she gets sick. Then you turn the knob again, and she gets betta. Get it?"

Judy turned the knob on the doll's head until a new face appeared. "She has measles!" said Stink.

"She talks when you hug her too." Judy hugged the doll.

"I have measles," said Hedda-Get-Betta.

Judy turned the knob until another face appeared. Then she hugged the doll again.

"I have chicken pox," said Hedda-Get-Betta.

"Cool," said Stink. "A sick doll. With three heads."

Judy turned the knob once more and hugged the doll. "All better," said Hedda.

"Can I make her get sick, then better?" asked Stink.

"No," said Judy. "I'm the doctor."

Judy opened her doctor kit. "At last I have someone to practice on," she said.

"You practice on me all the time," said Stink.

"Someone who doesn't complain."

"You'd complain too if you had to hold

up a lamp and get bandages all over you. Why can't I ever be Elizabeth Blackwell, First Woman Doctor?"

"For one thing, you're a boy."

"Can I put her arm in a sling?" asked Stink.

"No," said Judy. She held the ear scope up to Hedda's ear and turned on the light.

"Can I mix up some of this blood from your doctor kit?"

"Shh, I'm listening." She held the stethoscope on Hedda. Then she held it on Stink's chest. "Hmm."

"What?" said Stink. "What do you hear?"

"A heartbeat. This can mean only one thing."

"What?"

"You're alive!"

"Can I listen for a heartbeat?"

"Okay, okay. But first get me a glass of water to mix the blood in."

"You get it," said Stink.

"Don't touch anything until I get back," said Judy. "Don't even breathe."

As soon as Judy rounded the corner, Stink turned the knob on the doll's head. Measles. He turned the knob again. Chicken pox. Measles. Chicken pox. Measles. Chicken pox. Stink turned Hedda-Get-Betta's head back and forth, over and over, faster and faster.

"Uh-oh," said Stink.

"What?" Judy asked, returning with a sloshing glass of water.

"Her head is stuck," he said. Judy grabbed Hedda-Get-Betta away from Stink.

"I have chicken pox," Hedda said. Judy tried to turn the knob. The knob was stuck all right. It would not turn, no matter how hard Judy twisted and yanked and pulled. "I have chicken pox. I have chicken pox," Hedda said again and again.

"Her head is stuck on chicken pox!" Judy moaned.

"It's not my fault," said Stink.

"Is too! Now she'll never get better!" Judy took Hedda's pulse. She listened to Hedda's heart. She checked Hedda's forehead for a fever. "My first patient, and she's going to have chicken pox for the rest of her life!"

Judy took the doll to her mother. But Mom could not turn the knob, even with her best opening-pickle-jars twist. Judy took the doll to her father. But Dad could not get the doll's head to turn, even with his best opening-spaghetti-sauce turn.

"What are you going to do?" asked Dad.

"There's only one thing I can think of."

"Give her a shot?" asked Mom.

"No," said Judy. "Band-Aids!"

"Cool!" said Stink.

Stink and Judy put fancy Band-Aids on Hedda-Get-Betta's face, one for every chicken pock. Then they put Band-Aids all over her body. There were Endangered Species Band-Aids, Dinosaurs, Tattoos, Mermaids, and Race Cars. Even Glow-in-the-Dark Bloodshot-Eyeball Band-Aids.

"So she won't scratch," said Doctor Judy.

"I'm glad that emergency's over," Dad said.

Judy tried to turn the doll's head one last time. She did not yank or twist or pull. She very slowly, very carefully turned the knob. Hedda's head turned, and her smiling, no-chicken-pox face reappeared.

"I cured her!" Judy yelled. She hugged her doll. "All better," said Hedda-Get-Betta.

"Good as new," said Mom and Dad.

"I'm just glad she didn't have spotted fever," said Judy. "I never in a million years would have had enough Band-Aids for that!"

The T. P. Club

"I think it's going to rain for forty days and forty nights," said Stink.

Judy was hanging blankets from her top bunk to make a rain forest canopy over her bottom bunk. When that was done, she set Jaws on the top bunk for a jungly effect. Who needed a two-toed sloth? She climbed in and spread out her Me collage. Mouse climbed in after her. "Don't get hair on my collage," Judy warned her.

Stink stuck his head through the blankets.

"Who's that with hair sticking all out?" he asked, pointing to her collage.

"That's me in a bad mood on the first day of school."

"Where's me? Don't they need to know about brothers?"

"You mean *bothers?*" asked Judy.

She pointed to some dirt glued in the lower left-hand corner.

"I'm dirt?" asked Stink.

Judy cracked up. "That's for selling moon dust," said Judy.

"What's that blob? Blood?"

"Red. MY FAVORITE COLOR."

"Are those Spider Web Band-Aids?" Stink asked. "Where'd you get glitter glue? Can I come in there and glitter glue my bat wings?"

Her little brother, the bat freak, was becoming a regular Frank Pearl.

"There's no room, Stink. This is serious. I only have about two more weeks to finish."

Judy cut out a picture of Hedda from the ad in her *Luna Girls* magazine and pasted it in the doctor corner, right next to her drawing of Elizabeth Blackwell copied from an encyclopedia.

She checked Mr. Todd's list of collage ideas.

CLUBS. I don't belong to any clubs,

thought Judy. She'd have to skip that one.

HOBBIES. Collecting things was her favorite hobby. But she couldn't paste a scab or a Barbie head to the collage. She taped on the pizza table from her newest collection—the one Mr. Todd had given her.

THE WORST THING THAT EVER HAPPENED. She couldn't think of anything. Maybe the worst thing that ever happened to her hadn't happened yet.

THE FUNNIEST THING THAT EVER HAPPENED. When I knocked real spooky on the wall of Stink's room one night and scared him, she thought. But how could she put that on a collage?

Judy puzzled over her Me collage until the rain finally stopped. She called Rocky.

"Meet me at the manhole in five," she told him.

Rocky wore his boa constrictor shirt. Judy wore her boa constrictor shirt. "Same-same!" said Judy and Rocky, slapping hands together twice in a high-five, the way they always had when they did something exactly alike.

Judy and Rocky stood on the manhole. "What do you think is under the street?" asked Rocky.

"Oodles and oodles of worms," said Judy.

"Let's collect some in the street and throw them down there," said Rocky.

"Too oogley," said Judy.

"We could look for rainbows in puddles," Rocky suggested.

"Too hard!" said Judy.

"Listen," said Rocky. "I hear toads. We could catch toads!"

Rocky ran back home to get a bucket. When he came back, they cornered a toad and popped the bucket on top of it.

"Gotcha!" Judy held it in her hand. "It feels soft and bumpy. It's kind of cool, but not slimy."

All of a sudden, Judy felt something warm and wet in her hand. "Yuck!" she cried. "That toad peed on me." She tossed the toad back into the bucket.

"It's probably just wet from the rain," Rocky said.

"Oh, yeah? Then you pick it up." Rocky picked up the toad. He held it in his hand. It

felt soft and bumpy and cool-but-not-slimy all at once.

Just then Rocky felt something warm and wet in his hand. "Yuck," Rocky cried. "Now that toad peed on me." He tossed the toad back into the bucket.

"See what I mean?" said Judy. "I can't believe it happened to both of us the same!"

"Same-same!" said Rocky, and they double-high-fived. "Now it's like we're members of the same club. A secret club that only the two of us know about."

"And now we have a club to put on our Me collages," said Judy.

"What should we call it?" asked Rocky.

"The Toad Pee Club!"

"Rare!" said Rocky. "We could put T. P.

Club on our collages. People will think it stands for the Toilet Paper Club."

"Perfect," Judy said.

"Hey, what are you two doing?" asked Stink, running down the sidewalk in too-big boots.

"Nothing," said Judy, wiping her hands down the sides of her pants.

"Yes, you are," said Stink. "I can tell by your caterpillar eyebrow."

"What caterpillar eyebrow?"

"Your eyebrows make a fuzzy caterpillar when you don't want to tell me something." Judy Moody never knew she had caterpillar eyebrows before.

"Yeah, a stinging caterpillar," said Judy.

"We're starting a club," said Rocky.

"A secret club," Judy said quickly.

"I like secrets," said Stink. "I want to be in the club."

"You can't just be in the club," said Judy. "Something has to happen to you."

"I want the thing to happen to me too."

"No, you don't," said Judy.

"It's yucky," Rocky said.

"What?" asked Stink.

"Never mind," said Judy.

"You have to pick up that toad," Rocky told Stink.

"This is a trick, isn't it?" asked Stink. "To get me to pick up a slimy, bumpy old toad."

"That's right," said Judy.

Stink picked up the toad anyway. "Hey, it feels . . . interesting. Like a pickle. I never picked up a toad before," said Stink. "Now can I be in the club?"

"No," said Judy.

"I can't believe it's not slimy," said Stink.

"Just wait," said Rocky.

"I'm not going to get warts or anything, am I?"

"Do you feel anything?" asked Rocky.

"No," said Stink.

"Oh, well," said Judy. "Put the toad back. There. See? You can't be in the club."

Stink started to cry. "But I picked up the toad, and I want to be in the club."

"Don't cry," said Judy. "Trust me, Stink, you don't want to be in this club."

Just then Stink's eyes opened very wide. There was something warm and wet on his hand. Judy Moody and Rocky fell down laughing.

"Am I in the club yet?" asked Stink.

"Yes! Yes! Yes!" said Judy and Rocky. "The Toad Pee Club!"

"Yippee!" cried Stink. "I'm in the Toad Pee Club!"

The Worst Thing Ever

D-day. Doomsday. Dumbday. Saturday. The day of Frank Eats-Paste Pearl's birthday party. I'd rather eat ten jars of paste myself than go to that party, Judy thought.

For three whole weeks she had kept the hand-delivered-by-Frank-Pearl birthday invitation hidden inside the bottom of her Tip-It game, where Mom and Dad (who hated Tip-It) would NEVER find it.

Then today, the very day of the party, it happened. Dad found out.

She, Judy Moody, just had to ask Dad to take her to Fur & Fangs for some toad food. She just happened to be looking at a tadpole kit with real live frog eggs—*Watch tadpoles turn into frogs! See tails shrink, feet grow, legs form!*—hoping to talk Dad into buying it for her when another kit just like it bumped into her. Holding the kit was Frank's mom.

"Judy!" Frank's mom said. "Isn't that funny? It looks like we had the same idea for Frank's present! I thought he'd love watching a tadpole turn into a frog. I was about to buy him the same kit!"

"Um, I wasn't . . . I mean, you were?"

"Frank's really looking forward to seeing you at his party."

"Party?" Dad's ears perked up. "Whose party?"

"Frank's!" said his mom. "I'm Mrs. Pearl, Frank's mom."

"Nice to meet you," said Dad.

"Very nice to meet *you*," said Mrs. Pearl. "And Judy, I'll see you this afternoon. Bye for now."

Mrs. Pearl put the tadpole kit she was holding back on the shelf.

"Frank LOVES reptiles," she said.

Amphibians, thought Judy.

"Judy, why didn't you just say you needed to come here to get your friend a birthday present? Did I know you had a party to go to today?" Dad asked.

"No."

In the car, Judy tried to convince her Dad that there would be kids at the party making rude body noises and calling each other animal-breath names.

"You'll have fun."

"You know, Frank Pearl eats paste," said Judy.

"Look. You've already got the tadpole kit," Dad said.

"I was kind of sort of hoping I could keep it."

"But Mrs. Pearl put hers back when she saw yours. At least take it over, Judy."

"Do I have to wrap it?" asked Judy.

From the look on his face, she knew the answer.

Judy Moody wrapped the too-good-for-a-paste-eater present in boring newspaper (not the comics). Even though the party started at two o'clock, she told Mom and Dad that the party didn't start until four o'clock, so she would only have to go for the last disgusting minutes.

The whole family rode in the car to Frank Pearl's house. Even Toady went along, carried by Stink in a yogurt container. Judy held Frank's lumpy present and fell into a bad-mood back-seat slump. Why did Rocky have to go to his grandma's TODAY of all days?

"She's crying!" Stink reported to the front seat.

"Am not!" she said back with her best troll eyes ever.

"Wait here," Judy told her family when they got to Frank's house.

"Go ahead. Have fun," Dad said. "We'll be back for you in half an hour. Forty minutes tops."

"We're only going to the supermarket," said Mom. But they might as well have been going to New Zealand.

Mrs. Pearl answered the door. "Judy! We thought you'd changed your mind. C'mon out back."

"Fra-ank. Judy's here, honey," Mrs. Pearl called out to the backyard.

Judy looked around the yard. All she could see were boys. Boys hurling icing insects at each other and boys mixing chocolate cake with ketchup and boys conducting an experiment with Kool-Aid and a grasshopper.

"Where are the other kids?" asked Judy.

"Everybody's here, honey. Frank's little sister, Maggie, went off to a friend's. I think you know all the boys from school. And there's Adrian and Sandy from next door."

Sandy was a boy. So was Adrian. That

Frank Pearl had tricked her—the girls next door were boys! She, Judy Moody, was definitely the one and only girl. Alone. At Frank Pearl's all-boy-except-her birthday party!

Judy wanted to climb right up Frank Pearl's tire-swing rope and howl like a rain forest monkey. Instead she asked, "Do you have a bathroom?"

Judy decided to stay in the Pearls' bathroom forever. Or at least until her parents came back from New Zealand. Frank Pearl's all-boy party had to be THE WORST THING THAT EVER HAPPENED to her.

Judy looked for something to do. Uncapping an eyebrow pencil, she drew some sharp new teeth on her faded first-day-of-school shark T-shirt. Rare.

Knock knock.

"Ju-dy? Are you in there?" Judy turned on the water in a hurry so Mrs. Pearl would think she was washing her hands.

"Just a minute!" she called. Water sprayed her all over, soaking her shirt. The sharp new shark teeth blurred and ran.

Judy opened the door. Mrs. Pearl said, "Frank was about to open your present, but we couldn't find you."

Back outside, Brad pointed at Judy's wet shirt. "You guys! It's a shark! With black blood dripping from its mouth!"

"Cool!" "Wow!" "How'd you do that?"

"Talent," said Judy. "And water."

"Water fight!" Brad took a glass of water and threw it on Adam. Mitchell threw one at Dylan. Frank poured one right over his own head and grinned.

Mrs. Pearl whistled, which put a stop to the water battle. "Dylan! Brad! Your parents are here. Don't forget your party favors." Mrs. Pearl gave a baby Slinky to each kid as he went out the door. By the time she got to Judy, there were no more baby Slinkies left.

"I must have counted wrong," said Mrs. Pearl.

"Or Brad took two," said Frank.

"Here, Judy. I was going to buy these for party favors, but I couldn't find enough." Mrs. Pearl handed her a miniature rock-and-gem collection in a plastic see-through box! Tiny amethyst and jade stones. Even a crackly amber one.

"Thank you, Mrs. Pearl!" Judy said, and she meant it. "I love collecting stones and things. Once my brother thought he found a real moon rock!"

"Frank's a collector too," said Mrs. Pearl. "All the boys are gone, Frank. Why don't you take Judy up to your room and show her while she waits for her parents?"

"C'mon. Last one up's a rotten banana!" said Frank.

He probably collects paste jars, Judy thought. He probably eats it for a midnight snack.

Frank Pearl's shelves were lined with coffee cans and baby food jars. Each one was filled with marbles, rubber bugs, erasers, something. Judy couldn't help

asking, "Do you have any baseball erasers?"

"I have ten!" said Frank. "I got them FREE when a real Oriole came to the library."

"Really? Me too!" Judy smiled. She almost said "Same-same," then caught herself just in time.

"I'm taping one to my Me collage, beside my favorite bug, a click beetle, for HOBBIES—you know, collecting things."

"That's my hobby too," Judy told him.

He also had two pencil sharpeners—a Liberty Bell and a brain—and a teeny-tiny flip-book from Vic's. Frank Pearl showed her his buffalo nickel, which he kept in a double-locked piggy bank. "It's not really a collection yet because there's only one."

"That's okay," said Judy.

Frank also had a killer comic-book collection, with really old ones like the Green Hornet, Richie Rich, and Captain Marvel. To top it off, he even had a miniature soap collection, with fancy hotel names on the wrappers.

Judy forgot all about wanting to leave. "What's that?" she asked.

"A pitcher plant. It catches insects. They think it's a flower, so they land on it. Then they fall down this tube, and the plant eats them."

"Rare!" said Judy. "I have a Venus flytrap named Jaws."

"I know," said Frank. "That was funny when you brought it to school, how it ate that hamburger and stunk up your backpack and everything."

"Fra-ank! Ju-dy! The Moodys are here."

"I guess I gotta go," Judy told Frank.

"Well, thanks for the tadpole kit," Frank said, twisting a leg of the rubber click beetle from his collection.

"Hey, do you really eat paste?" asked Judy.

"I tasted it one time. For a dare."

"Rare!" Judy said.

Definitely the Worst Thing Ever

Judy's day was off to a grouchy start. This was the day that Stink, her once smelly, sold-dirt-for-moon-dust brother was going with his class to Washington, D.C., to see the president's house!

She found out Mom and Dad were going too, as chaperones.

Yours Truly had to stay home and finish her Me collage. She, Judy Moody, still had several bald spots to fill.

"I think my brain has a leak," Judy told her family. "I can't think of one more interesting thing to put on my collage."

Judy sank down on the family-room couch like a balloon that had lost three days' air. "Interesting things could happen to me better in Washington, D.C.," said Judy.

"You know it's just for the second-grade classes, honey," said Mom.

"ROAR!" was all she said.

"We might be home late," Dad told her. "You can go to Rocky's after school. You two can finish up your projects together."

"You'll have fun," said Mom. "And aren't you going to an assembly today for Brush Your Teeth Week?"

How could she forget? One more reason to be grouchy. Stink got to rub elbows with the president while she, Judy Moody, would be shaking the hands of Mr. Tooth and Mrs. Floss.

Stink waddled into the family room wrapped in a red and white striped tablecloth, looking like he just got hit by a flying picnic.

"What's that?" asked Judy.

"It's a costume, for my YOU ARE THE FLAG project. I'm the flag."

"Stink, you're not supposed to *be* the flag. You're supposed to tell what the flag means to you."

"To me it means I *am* the flag."

"What's on your head?"

"A hat. See, each star is a state, like on the flag. There's one for all forty-eight states."

"Guess what. There are fifty states, Stink."

"Nuh-uh. I counted. I crossed them off on my map."

"Count again," Judy said. "You probably forgot Hawaii and Alaska."

"Do you think the president will notice?" asked Stink.

"Stink, the president just about made the states. He'll notice."

"Okay, okay. I'll stick two more on."

"Every other second-grader writes a flag poem or draws a picture for YOU ARE THE FLAG. *My* brother's a human flag."

"What's wrong with that?"

"You look like a star-spangled mummy and walk like a banana. That's what."

"I get to see a room where everything is made of real gold. Even the curtains and bedspreads. Heather Strong says the lamps are made of diamonds."

"Heather Strong lies," said Judy.

It was no use. She would have to change her Me collage. Frank's birthday party was no longer THE WORST THING EVER. Frank Pearl ate paste for a dare! And he gave her a baby food jar with six ants and a fly for Jaws.

Not meeting the president of her own United fifty States was absolutely and positively THE WORST THING THAT EVER

HAPPENED. Her whole family, including her brother, the human flag, was going to Washington, D.C., while she, Judy Moody, would be listening to a talking tooth.

The Funniest Thing Ever

It was pouring outside. Judy's dad would not let her leave for school without an umbrella, and the only one she could find was her first-grade yellow ducky one. She wouldn't open a baby umbrella, so she got soaked clear through. The sun is probably shining over the president's house this second, thought Judy. She felt like a bike left out in the rain.

"Frank wants to come over after school too," Rocky told her on the bus. "And I have a brand new ten-dollar bill from Nay-Nay. We can go to Vic's after school and buy something really rare."

"Do they have any real gold at Vic's?" was all she said.

In Spelling, Judy wrote WEASELS when Mr. Todd had really said MEASLES. In Science, when Jessica Finch threw Judy the ball of yarn for their giant spider web, she dropped it. It rolled out the door just when Ms. Tuxedo, the principal, walked past in high heels. And at the Brush Your Teeth Week assembly, Mr. Tooth picked Judy to be a cavity. On stage. In front of the whole school.

She could not get her mind off Stink at the president's house, where *she* wasn't. Seeing all that real gold. Would he get to shake the president's hand? Meet the president's daughter? Sit in a gold chair?

"Are flags allowed to talk?" she asked Frank.

"Only if they're talking flags!"

That did it. There would be no living with Stink once he had been to the president's.

On the bus ride home, Rocky squirted Frank with his magic nickel. Frank snorted, wiping the drips on his sleeve. Judy pretended it was funny. Really she was thinking, Stink could be petting the president's puppy, right now, this very instant. When

Rocky said, "I can't wait to go to Vic's," Judy grunted.

The three of them half-ran through leftover puddles all the way to Vic's. Rocky didn't even stop to cross through China and Japan the right way. "What's the big hurry?" she asked.

"I need something," said Rocky, "but there's only one left, and I want to make sure I get it!" he said. When they got to Vic's, Rocky went straight to the counter.

"Over here," Rocky told them. "There's still one left!"

Judy stood on tiptoes to look in a box on top of the counter. Lying in the bottom was . . . a hand. A person's hand! Judy almost screamed. Frank almost screamed too. Then they realized it was made out of rubber.

"What do you think?" asked Rocky.

"Rare," said Judy.

"Ace," said Frank. "It looks so real. Fingernails and everything!"

Rocky bought the hand and three fireballs.

"What are you going to do with your hand?" Frank asked.

"I don't know," said Rocky. "I just like it."

When they got to Rocky's house, Judy tried to work on her Me collage. But she was not in a FUNNIEST THING EVER mood. All the funny stuff that had ever happened to her seemed to have gotten up and left. Marched right out of her brain like a line of ants from a picnic.

Rocky showed Judy and Frank his finished collage. "Here's Thomas Jefferson in the window of my house for WHERE I LIVE. I cut him out of play money."

"That's good!" said Frank. "For Jefferson Street."

"The piece of cloth is part of my sling from when I broke my arm, THE WORST THING EVER."

"And here's a toilet paper roll for the T. P. Club, a secret club I'm in," Rocky said, glancing at Judy.

"What kind of club has toilet paper?" asked Frank.

"If I tell you, it won't be a secret,"

"Who's this?" Frank asked Rocky, pointing to a lizard.

"Houdini, MY FAVORITE PET."

"And who's that guy, walking through a brick wall?" Frank asked.

"That's my favorite part. My mom made a copy of a picture of the real Harry Houdini from a library book."

Judy touched a clump of garlic. "Are you trying to scare away vampires or something?"

"That's from one time when I ate a whole thing of garlic by mistake. THE FUNNIEST THING EVER was that I stunk like a skunk for a week!"

"Like Jaws when it ate that hamburger!" said Frank.

"Like Stink when he takes his smelly shoes off," said Judy.

"Is this you?" Frank asked.

"That's me in my magician hat, making a fishbowl disappear."

"Too bad you can't make Stink disappear," said Judy.

"Too bad I'm done," said Rocky. "It would have been really funny to put the rubber hand on my collage."

That's when it happened. An idea. The funniest of all funnies. It orbited Judy's head and landed like a spaceship, the way good ideas do.

"Rocky! You're a genius! Let's go to my

house," Judy said. "And bring the hand."

"You're *not* a genius," said Rocky. "Nobody's home at your house. We could get into all kinds of trouble."

"Exactly!" said Judy. "C'mon. There's a key hidden in the gutter pipe."

"Did you forget something?" asked Frank.

"Yes," Judy said. "I forgot to play a trick on Stink!"

Once inside, Judy raced around her house, looking for the perfect spot to leave the hand, a place where Stink would be sure to find it right away. The couch? Toady's aquarium? The refrigerator? Under his pillow?

The bathroom!

Or here?

Maybe here?

I've got it!

Perfect!

In the downstairs bathroom, Judy lifted up the toilet seat, just a crack, and perched the hand there, its fingernails hanging over the edge. "It looks real," said Rocky.

"This will scare the president right out of him," said Judy. "For sure."

Back at Rocky's, Judy, Frank, and Rocky knelt on Rocky's bed, looking out the window. Every time a car zoomed by on Jefferson Street, they yelled, "It's them!" Finally Judy saw a blue van, for real. "Run!" she yelled. "They're pulling into the driveway!"

Stink was so excited telling Judy, Rocky, and Frank all about the president's house that Hawaii and Alaska fell off his hat.

Why doesn't he go to the bathroom? thought Judy.

"There's a movie theater—I swear! Inside the president's house. And a room with a secret door. No lie. Even a clock that tells you when it's time to take a bath," said Stink.

"Rare!" said Judy. "You need one of those."

Go into the bathroom, Stink, she wished silently. As if he had heard, Stink stopped his story. Balancing his hat on his head, he walked into the bathroom and shut the door behind him. The lock clicked.

Mom and Dad asked Judy about the Mr. Tooth assembly, but her ears were tuned to the bathroom. "AAAAAHHHHH!" screamed Stink. He burst out of the bathroom, hat crashing to the floor, stars flying.

"Hey! Dad! Mom! There's somebody in the toilet!"

Judy Moody, Rocky, and Frank Pearl fell on the floor laughing.

The Me Collage

Stink watched Judy finish her collage after school the next day. "Almost done," said Judy. "It's due tomorrow."

Stink pointed. "You still have a bald spot right there next to the picture of Jaws."

Judy carefully taped a doll hand from her collection over the empty space. "Not anymore," she said.

"That hand? Is it for the trick you played on me?" asked Stink.

"Yes. It's THE FUNNIEST THING EVER," said Judy, with a grin.

"You mean you're going to tell your whole class I thought there was somebody in our toilet?"

"Stink, I'm making you famous."

"Couldn't you change my name or something?" asked Stink.

"Or something," said Judy.

When Judy got up the next morning, it was pouring rain again. Something told her to get ready for a bad-mood Friday.

"Let's put your Me collage in a garbage bag so it won't get wet," Dad suggested when she brought it downstairs.

"Dad, I'm not carrying my Me collage in a garbage bag."

"Why not?"

"Did Van Gogh put his *Starry Night* in a garbage bag?"

"She's got a point there," said Mom.

"Garbage bags probably hadn't been invented yet," said Dad. "If Van Gogh had garbage bags, believe me, he would have been smart enough to use them."

"Honey, why don't you take the bus, and Dad'll bring your collage to school after he takes Stink to the dentist?" Mom said. "Stink's taking Toady to school today, so Dad has to drop him off anyway."

"I want to take my collage to school myself. That way I can be sure nothing will happen to it."

"What could happen to it?" asked Mom.

"There could be a tornado," said Stink, "and the wind could make you drop it, and it could get run over by a bus."

"Hardee, har, har," said Judy.

"You do have a lot of other stuff to carry," said her dad. Judy had her lunch, her dad's lab coat so she could dress like a doctor for her talk, Hedda-Get-Betta, her doctor kit, and plenty of Band-Aids.

"Okay," she said, "but don't squish anything and don't get it wet and it has to be there by eleven o'clock and don't let Stink do *anything*." She gave her brother her best troll-eyes stare.

"We'll be careful," said Dad.

Judy rode the bus with Rocky, who

practiced his Squirting Nickel magic trick on her for the one-hundredth time.

"Okay! It works!" Judy told him, wiping drips from her face. Rocky cracked up.

All morning, Judy imagined things happening to her collage. What if it fell into a puddle when her father opened the car door? What if Toady got out of Stink's pocket and peed on the collage? What if a tornado came, like Stink said . . .

Eleven o'clock came, and her collage still was not there. No sign of Stink. Or Dad.

Judy could hardly listen to the other kids showing their Me collages. She kept her eyes glued to the door of 3T.

"Judy, would you like to go next?" asked Mr. Todd, startling her.

"I'd like to go last," said Judy.

"Frank?"

"I'd like to go last too," said Frank. "After Judy."

Judy looked at Frank's desk. "Where's your Me collage?" she asked him.

"I didn't bring it. I mean, I'm not finished. I still don't have a CLUB," Frank whispered. "Where's yours?"

"My brother's supposed to bring it," said Judy. She glanced at the door again. There he was! Stink motioned for her to come out in the hall.

Stink looked sick. "What's wrong?" Judy asked.

"If I tell you," said Stink, "you'll be in the worst mood ever."

"Where is it?" asked Judy. "Did you drop my collage in a puddle? Did Toady pee on it?"

"No," said Stink. "Not that."

"Where is it?" she asked again.

"Dad's in the boys' room. Drying it off."

Judy ran down to the boys' room, pushed the door open, and went right in. Crumpled paper towels were everywhere. "Dad!"

"Judy!"

"Is it ruined? Let me see!"

Dad held up her collage. Right smack dab in the center was a big purple stain the size of a pancake. Not a silver dollar one either. A giant, jaggedy triangle — a grape-colored lake floating in the middle of her collage!

"What happened?" Judy yelled.

"I was drinking Jungle Juice from a box," said Stink, standing behind her in the doorway, "and trying this thing with my straw. . . . I'm sorry."

"Stink! You wrecked it. Dad! How could you let him drink Jungle Juice in the car?"

"Look, it's not that bad," he said. "It almost looks like it's supposed to be there. I'll speak with Mr. Todd. Maybe he'll let you have the weekend and we can fix it. Cover it up somehow."

"Maybe we can erase it," said Stink. "With a giant eraser."

"Let me see." Judy held up the collage, looking it over. Even with the purple stain, she could still see the rain forest with Doctor

Judy Moody in the very middle. And none of the Band-Aids had come off.

"Never mind," said Judy.

"Never mind?" asked Dad.

"It's okay," she said. "At least it didn't get run over by a bus in a tornado."

"It's okay?" asked Stink. "You mean you're not going to put a rubber foot in my bed or anything?"

"No," said Judy. She grinned at her brother. "But that is a good idea."

"Look, honey. I know you worked forever on this. We'll make it up to you somehow."

"I know what to do. Stink, let me have your black marker." They all went out into the hall, and Stink dug a marker out of his backpack. Judy set the collage on the floor and drew a black outline around the big purple triangle.

"Are you cuckoo?" asked Stink. "That's just going to make it stand out more."

"That's what I want," said Judy. "Then it'll look like it was supposed to be there all the time."

"I'm proud of you, Judy," said Dad. "The

way you took an accident like this and turned it into something good."

"What's it supposed to be?" Stink asked.

"Virginia," she said. "The state of Pocahontas and Thomas Jefferson. The place WHERE I LIVE."

Band-Aids and Ice Cream

When Judy got back to class, she put on her doctor coat, walked to the front of the room, and held her Me collage high. She stood tall, as if her brother had not nearly ruined her masterpiece with Jungle Juice. She tried to look like a person who would grow up to be a doctor and make the world a better place. A person who could turn a bad mood right around.

Judy told about herself and her family, including the time Stink sold moon dust, which explained why her brother was a piece of dirt. She traced the outline of Virginia with her finger to show where she lived. She talked about Rocky, her best friend, and Frank, her new friend. She pointed to a paste jar lid taped to a corner and told the class that Frank ate paste for a dare once.

"Is that Jaws?" asked Brad. "The thing that eats bugs?"

"Yes," said Judy. "Even though I have a cat, Jaws is MY FAVORITE PET. When I grow up and become a doctor, I want to move to the rain forest and search for medicines in rare plants that could cure ucky diseases."

Judy pointed out the pizza table from Mr. Todd and other stuff she collected for HOBBIES. She told the class that she was a member of the T. P. Club, but that she couldn't tell them what T. P. stood for.

"This is a picture my parents took of Stink, standing outside the White House in his flag costume." And she explained why it was THE WORST THING THAT EVER HAPPENED to her. Everybody's favorite part of her collage was when she showed the doll hand, coming out of a magazine toilet. So Judy told them about how the worst thing ever turned into THE FUNNIEST THING EVER.

"Any questions?" she asked the class.

"Who's the old lady?" asked Frank.

Judy explained about Elizabeth Blackwell, First Woman Doctor, and then gave a demonstration of her doctor skills. She put Rocky's arm in a sling and wrapped bandages around Frank's knee. She pulled out her pretend blood, and used Hedda-Get-Betta to show how to apply Band-Aids.

"That's it. Me. Judy Moody."

"Great job, Judy," said Mr. Todd. "Class, any comments?"

"I like how you painted Virginia in the middle of your collage to show where you live," said Jessica Finch, "instead of just using a picture of your house."

"Those Tattoo Band-Aids are the coolest," said Dylan. "I have a blister. Can I have one?"

"I have a hangnail!"

"I have a paper cut!"

"I have a mosquito bite!"

Before Judy knew it, everybody in the whole class was wearing Tattoo Band-Aids.

"Judy Moody, you're a mover and a shaker," said Mr. Todd.

"I am?" asked Judy. "What's that mean?"

Mr. Todd laughed. "Let's just say it means you have imagination."

What had almost become a bad-mood Friday had turned into one very fine day.

And it wasn't over yet.

When she walked out to get the bus that afternoon, Mom and Dad were waiting to take Judy and Stink for ice cream at Screamin' Mimi's.

"I'm getting that blue ice cream, Rain Forest Mist. Like you guys always do!" Stink jumped up and down, holding his pocket with the toad.

"Did your teacher like Toady?" Judy asked.

"Yes, but she was almost in the Toad Pee Club," said Stink. Judy cracked up.

"Mom, Dad, can I ask Rocky and Frank to come too?"

"That's a great idea," Mom said.

Outside Screamin' Mimi's, Judy licked

her Rain Forest Mist scoop on top of Chocolate Mud, her favorite. She was in her best Judy Moody mood ever.

Stink took Toady out of his pocket and set him on the picnic table. Toady hopped toward a blue drip from Rocky's ice cream cone.

"Toady likes Rain Forest Mist!" said Rocky.

"Hey, Frank," Judy asked, "when are you going to finish your Me collage?"

"Mr. Todd said I could bring it on Monday."

"You're not done yet?" asked Rocky.

"I *still* don't have anything for CLUBS. The dictionary says a club is three or more people."

Judy looked at Rocky. Rocky looked at Stink. Stink looked at Judy. All three of them looked at Frank.

"If you pick up Toady right now, you can be in a club," said Judy.

"Really?" asked Frank.

"Really and truly," said Judy and Rocky at the same time.

Frank crinkled his nose. "I don't get it."

Rocky laughed. "You will."

Frank scooped up Toady with one hand.

"Use both hands," said Judy.

"Like this," said Rocky, cupping his hands.

"Just hold him a minute," said Stink.

"I still don't get it," said Frank.

"Oh, you'll *get* it," said Judy, Rocky, and Stink.

A second later, Frank felt something warm and wet in his hand. He crossed his eyes, and they all fell down laughing.

Megan McDonald

is the award-winning author of the Judy Moody series. She says that most of Judy's stories "grew out of anecdotes about growing up with my four sisters." She confesses, "I *am* Judy Moody. Same-same! In my family of sisters, we're famous for exaggeration. Judy Moody is me . . . exaggerated." Megan McDonald lives with her husband in northern California.

Peter H. Reynolds

says he felt an immediate connection to Judy Moody because, "having a daughter, I have witnessed firsthand the adventures of a very independent-minded girl." Peter H. Reynolds lives in Massachusetts, just down the street from his twin brother.

Praise for Judy Moody

A *New York Times* Bestseller

An American Library Association Notable Children's Book

A New York Public Library 100 Titles for Reading and Sharing Selection

A *Publishers Weekly* Best Children's Book of the Year

A *Booklist* Notable Children's Book

★ "McDonald's comical novel introduces the entertainingly mercurial Judy Moody." — *Publishers Weekly* (starred review)

"Judy is independent, feisty, and full of energy, a delightful new character for beginning chapter-book readers." — *School Library Journal*

"Surefire fare for Cleary, Kline, and Hurwitz fans."
— *Kirkus Reviews*

DOUBLE RARE!
Judy Moody has her own website!

Come visit **www.judymoody.com**
for the latest in all things Judy Moody, including:

- ◉ All you need to know about the best-ever Judy Moody Fan Club

- ◉ Answers to all your V.I.Q.s (very important questions) about Judy

- ◉ Way-not-boring stuff about Megan McDonald and Peter H. Reynolds

- ◉ Double-cool activities that will be sure to put you in a mood — and not a bad mood, a good mood!

- ◉ Totally awesome T.P. Club info!

Be sure to read Judy's next adventure!

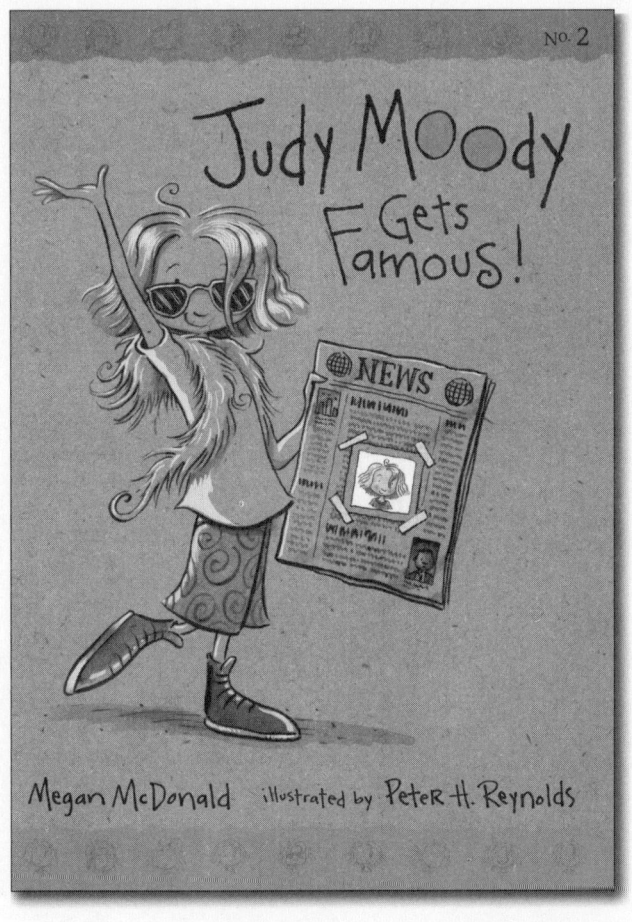

Turn the page for an excerpt. . . .

Since Jessica had become Queen Bee with the word *artichoke*, Judy decided to skip the dictionary and spell all the vegetables in the refrigerator instead.

"Do we have any artichokes?" Judy asked her mother, opening the door of the fridge.

"Since when did you start liking artichokes?" asked Mom.

"Don't worry, I'm not going to eat them or anything," said Judy. "It's for Spelling."

"Spelling?" Stink asked.

"Mr. Todd does have some creative ways of teaching Spelling," said Mom.

"Never mind," said Judy, giving up when she saw asparagus. Vegetables were too hard to spell. There had to be a food group that was easier.

At dinner Judy slurped up a noodle and asked, "How do you spell *spaghetti*?"

"N-O-O-D-L-E," said Stink.

"S-P-A-G-H-E-T-T-I," said Dad.

"Or P-A-S-T-A," said Mom.

"Never mind," said Judy. "Please pass the B-R-E-A-D."

"How was school today?" Mom asked.

"W-E-L-L," Judy said. "Jessica Finch won a T-I-A-R-A in a spelling bee and got her picture in the P-A-P-E-R. Even if she does look like an A-A-R-D-W-O-L-F, aardwolf."

"So that's what all this spelling is about," said Mom.

"You're W-E-I-R-D," Stink told his sister.

"*I* comes before *E*, Stink. Except after *C*. Everybody knows *that*." What a meatloaf.

"Actually," said Mom, "your brother's right."

"WHAT?" said Judy. "How can he be right? He broke the rule!"

"Lots of rules have exceptions,"

said Dad. "Times when you have to break the rule."

"No fair!" Judy slumped down in her chair. She was not going to become famous by spelling, that was for sure. The three strings of spaghetti left on her plate made the shape of a mean face. Judy made a mean face back.

Dad took a bite out of his garlic bread and asked Judy, "You're not in one of your famous moods again, are you?"

Look out, Judy Moody!

Stink

is starring in his very own series!

Catch Judy Moody's little brother in

Stink: The Incredible Shrinking Kid

by Megan McDonald, illustrated by Peter H. Reynolds

Here's a sneak peek at Stink's first adventure....

When Stink woke up the next morning, his bed felt as big as a country. The ceiling was up there with the sky. And it was a long way down to the floor.

When he went to brush his teeth, even the sink seemed too tall.

"Yipe! I really am shrinking," said Stink, checking himself out in the mirror. Were his arms a little shorter? Was his head a little smaller?

An excerpt from *Stink: The Incredible Shrinking Kid*

Stink got dressed. He put on up-and-down-striped pants and an up-and-down-striped shirt.

"What's with the stripes?" asked Judy.

"Makes me look taller," said Stink.

"If you say so," said Judy.

"What?"

"If you really want to look taller, here's what you do." Judy handed him a fancy shampoo-type bottle. "Put this hair gel on your hair and leave it in for ten minutes. Then you'll be able to comb your hair so it sticks straight up. Sticking-up hair will make you look taller."

Stink put the goopy goop in his hair. He left it in his hair while he made his bed. He left it in his hair while he packed up his backpack. He left it in his hair all through breakfast.

"We could play baseball, and you could be *short*stop," Judy told him.

"So funny I forgot to laugh," said Stink.

Judy pointed to Stink's hair. "Hey,

I think it's working!" she said.

"Really? Do you think people will notice?"

"They'll notice," said Judy.

Stink ran upstairs to look in the mirror. "HEY! My HAIR! It's ORANGE!"

"Don't worry," said Judy. "It'll wash out . . . in about a week."

"I look like a carrot!" said Stink.

"Carrots are tall," said Judy, and she laughed all the way to the bus stop.

An excerpt from *Stink: The Incredible Shrinking Kid*

#1 **Stink** the Incredible Shrinking Kid
Megan McDonald
illustrated by Peter H. Reynolds

#2 **Stink** and the Incredible Super-Galactic Jawbreaker
Megan McDonald
illustrated by Peter H. Reynolds

#3 **Stink** and the World's Worst Super-Stinky Sneakers
Megan McDonald
illustrated by Peter H. Reynolds

Be sure to check out
Stink's adventures!

Experience all of Judy Moody's moods!

Judy Moody Gets Famous!

Books by Megan McDonald and Peter H. Reynolds:

#1 – *Judy Moody*
#2 – *Judy Moody Gets Famous!*
#3 – *Judy Moody Saves the World!*
#4 – *Judy Moody Predicts the Future*
#5 – *Judy Moody, M.D.: The Doctor Is In!*
#6 – *Judy Moody Declares Independence*
#1 – *Stink: The Incredible Shrinking Kid*
#2 – *Stink and the Incredible Super-Galactic Jawbreaker*
#3 – *Stink and the World's Worst Super-Stinky Sneakers*
Judy Moody & Stink: The Holly Joliday
The Judy Moody Mood Journal
Judy Moody's Double-Rare Way-Not-Boring Book of Fun Stuff to Do

Books by Megan McDonald:
Ant and Honey Bee: What a Pair!
The Sisters Club

Books by Peter H. Reynolds:
The Dot
Ish
So Few of Me

Judy Moody Gets Famous!

Megan McDonald

illustrated by
Peter H. Reynolds

CANDLEWICK PRESS
CAMBRIDGE, MASSACHUSETTS

Text copyright © 2001 by Megan McDonald
Illustrations copyright © 2001 by Peter H. Reynolds
Judy Moody font copyright © 2004 by Peter H. Reynolds

Judy Moody®. Judy Moody is a registered trademark
of Candlewick Press, Inc.

All rights reserved. No part of this book may be reproduced,
transmitted, or stored in an information retrieval system in any form
or by any means, graphic, electronic, or mechanical, including
photocopying, taping, and recording, without prior written
permission from the publisher.

First paperback edition in this format 2006

The Library of Congress has cataloged the hardcover edition as follows:

McDonald, Megan.
Judy Moody gets famous! / Megan McDonald ;
illustrated by Peter Reynolds. —1st ed.
p. cm.
Summary: When a third-grade classmate gets her picture in
the paper for winning a spelling bee, Judy is determined
to find a way to become famous herself.
ISBN 978-0-7636-0849-1 (hardcover)
[1. Fame—Fiction. 2. Brothers and sisters—Fiction.]
I. Reynolds, Peter, ill. II. Title.
PZ7.M478419 Jv 2001
[Fic]—dc21   00-024200

ISBN 978-0-7636-1931-2 (paperback)

12 14 16 18 20 19 17 15 13 11

Printed in the United States of America

This book was typeset in Stone Informal.
The illustrations were done in watercolor, tea, and ink.

Candlewick Press
2067 Massachusetts Avenue
Cambridge, Massachusetts 02140

visit us at www.candlewick.com

For Kendra and Mary Lee
—M. M.

For Mum and Dad
—P. H. R.

Table of Contents

How Do You Spell Famous? ... 1

The Moody Hall of Fame 13

Infamous 23

Fame Is the Pits 40

Famous Pet Contest 55

Broken Records 73

Broken Parts 86

Body Parts 98

Judy Moody and Jessica Finch .. 106

Judy Moody, Superhero ... 119

Who's Who

Roar!
Star of the show,
famous for her
many moods.

Judy's father.
Good at crossword
puzzles, quiz shows,
and garage sales.

Judy's mother.
Former glee club
member. Knows her
vegetables.

Judy's scene-stealing
younger brother and star
of the Moody Hall of Fame.

Mouse

Judy's cat. Amazing contestant in the Fur & Fangs Famous Pet Contest.

Rocky

Judy's best friend since FOREVER and owner of a disappearing Superman ring.

Mr. Todd

Judy's teacher, a.k.a. Mr. Toad, world's greatest third-grade teacher.

Frank

Judy's paste-eating friend and one quarter of a human centipede.

Jessica

Judy's classmate, Jessica *Aardwolf* Finch, a.k.a. Know-it-all Queen of the Spelling Bee.

How Do You Spell Famous?

Judy Moody marched into third grade on a plain old Thursday, in a plain old ordinary mood. That was *before* Judy got stung by the Queen Bee.

Judy sat down at her desk, in the front row next to Frank Pearl.

"Hey, did you see Jessica Finch?" asked Frank in a low voice.

"Yeah, so? I see her every day. She sits catty-cornered behind me."

"She's wearing a crown."

Judy turned to look at Jessica, then whispered to Frank, "Where'd she get that? Burger Barn?"

"I don't know," said Frank. "Ask her. She says it's bejeweled."

"Well, it looks be-dumb, if you ask me," said Judy, though secretly she admired the sparkling ruby-like gems.

"Hey, are those real rubies?" Judy asked Jessica.

"They're costume jewelry," Jessica said.

"Who are you dressing up as? The Queen of England?"

"No, I'm the Queen Bee," said Jessica. "I won the N. V. Spelling Bee on Saturday."

"The envy spelling bee?" Judy asked.

Judy didn't envy anybody who had to spell long words into a microphone with a million and one people staring bug-eyed at her. She knew those people were silently yelling *FLUB IT UP* because they wanted their own kid to win.

"Not *envy*. N. V. As in Northern Virginia."

"Oh," said Judy. "Is that where you got the crown?"

"It's a tiara," said Jessica. "T-I-A-R-A. A tiara is a fancy crown like the Queen of England wears. Queen of the Bee has to know tons of definitions."

"What word did you win for?" Judy asked. "Frank wants to know," she added, in case Jessica thought *she* was interested.

"*Artichoke*. It's a fourth-grade word."

Artichoke! Judy could barely spell *meatloaf! Give me S-C-I-E-N-C-E any day*, she thought. Was that the rule? *I* before *E*? Or was it *E* before *I*?

"I have spelling posters in my room at home," said Jessica. "With all the rules. I even have a glow-in-the-dark one."

"That would give me spelling nightmares. I'll take my glow-in-the-dark skeleton poster any day. It shows all two hundred and six bones in the body!"

"Judy," said Mr. Todd. "The back of your head is not nearly as interesting as the front. And so far I've seen more of it today than I'd like."

"Sorry," said Judy, facing front again.

Jessica tapped Judy and passed her a folded page from the newspaper. Right there, SMACK-DAB in the MIDDLE of the newspaper for the whole world to see, was a picture of Jessica Finch. It even said LOCAL GIRL BECOMES QUEEN BEE in big fat headline letters.

"My dad says I got my fifteen minutes of fame," Jessica whispered to the back of Judy's head.

Judy did not turn around. She was green with N-V. Jessica A. Finch, Queen of the Dictionary, Class 3T, was famous! Judy could not help thinking how stupendous it would feel to be able to spell better than *meatloaf* and be the Queen Bee and wear a tiara. To get her own picture in the paper!

But she, Judy Moody, felt about as famous as a pencil.

☙ ☙ ☙

As soon as Judy got home from school, she decided to memorize the dictionary. But she got stuck on *aardwolf*. Three lousy words. Who ever heard of an aard*wolf* anyway? Silly old termite-eater. It had a pointy little head and beady little eyes and a pinched-up face that looked just like . . . Jessica A. Finch! Jessica *Aardwolf* Finch might be famous, but she was also a silly old termite-eater.

Since Jessica had become Queen Bee with the word *artichoke*, Judy decided to skip the dictionary and spell all the vegetables in the refrigerator instead.

"Do we have any artichokes?" Judy asked her mother, opening the door of the fridge.

"Since when did you start liking artichokes?" asked Mom.

"Don't worry, I'm not going to eat them or anything," said Judy. "It's for Spelling."

"Spelling?" Stink asked.

"Mr. Todd does have some creative ways of teaching Spelling," said Mom.

"Never mind," said Judy, giving up when she saw asparagus. Vegetables were too

hard to spell. There had to be a food group that was easier.

At dinner Judy slurped up a noodle and asked, "How do you spell *spaghetti*?"

"N-O-O-D-L-E," said Stink.

"S-P-A-G-H-E-T-T-I," said Dad.

"Or P-A-S-T-A," said Mom.

"Never mind," said Judy. "Please pass the B-R-E-A-D."

"How was school today?" Mom asked.

"W-E-L-L," Judy said. "Jessica Finch won a T-I-A-R-A in a spelling bee and got her picture in the P-A-P-E-R. Even if she does look like an A-A-R-D-W-O-L-F, aardwolf."

"So that's what all this spelling is about," said Mom.

"You're W-E-I-R-D," Stink told his sister.

"*I* comes before *E*, Stink. Except after *C*. Everybody knows *that*." What a meatloaf.

"Actually," said Mom, "your brother's right."

"WHAT?" said Judy. "How can he be right? He broke the rule!"

"Lots of rules have exceptions," said Dad. "Times when you have to break the rule."

"No fair!" Judy slumped down in her chair. She was not going to become famous by spelling, that was for sure. The three strings of spaghetti left on her plate made the shape of a mean face. Judy made a mean face back.

Dad took a bite out of his garlic bread

and asked Judy, "You're not in one of your famous moods again, are you?"

The Moody Hall of Fame

The next day at breakfast, Judy ate her corn flakes without even spelling them.

There had to be lots of ways people got famous besides spelling.

While she munched, Judy watched her little brother, Stink, hang stuff up on the refrigerator: his report card, the self-portrait that made him look like a monkey, and a photo of himself in his flag costume, from the time he went to Washington, D. C.,

without her. Above everything, he had spelled MOODY HALL OF FAME with letter magnets.

"Hey!" she said. "Where's me?"

"*I* made it," said Stink.

"Why not leave Judy some room, honey," said Mom. "She can hang things there too."

Judy ran back up the stairs, two by two. She searched her desk for things to put in the Moody Hall of Fame. But all she could find were rumpled-up papers, acorn hats, a year-old candy heart that said HOT STUFF, and a drawer full of pink dust from all the times she had erased her spelling words and brushed them into her top drawer.

She rummaged through her closet next. All she had there were her collections: Band-Aids, fancy toothpicks, body parts (from dolls!), Bazooka Joe comics, pizza tables. Forget it. A person could not be in a hall of fame for toothpicks and Band-Aids.

Then Judy remembered her scrapbox. Most kids, like Stink, had a scrapbook. What Judy had was a shoebox that smelled like old rubber. She stood on a chair and lifted the box down from the top shelf.

A lock of baby hair! A tooth she lost in first grade. Mom and Dad would never let her hang dead hair up on the fridge. And nobody wanted to see an old yellow tooth every time they opened the refrigerator. Judy came across a macaroni picture of herself in kindergarten, with a screaming O for a mouth. She put it back. Stink would just love the chance to call her a noodle head. And remind her that she had a big mouth.

Where were her report cards? There had to be some good ones. Certificates? Blue ribbons? She must have won something, sometime. But all she found were baby footprints, half-melted birthday candles, and dopey drawings of people with four eyes that she'd scribbled in preschool.

What about pictures of herself?

Pictures! Judy flipped through some old photos in an envelope. She had to find something as good as the picture of Stink the time he met the president. Here she

was with Santa Claus. But Santa looked like he was snoring. And there she was standing next to Abraham Lincoln (cardboard). No way could she be in the Moody Hall of Fame for having her picture taken with a cardboard president.

Then there was the one where she was facedown on the neighbor's driveway, throwing a tantrum, because she did NOT want to get her picture taken.

It was no use. Judy could not think of a single thing famous enough for the Moody Hall of Fame.

Judy went back down to the kitchen. The letter magnets on the fridge should have said THE STINK HALL OF FAME.

"So? Where's your stuff?" Stink asked.

"Did you leave it upstairs or something?"

"Or something," said Judy. She hadn't even found the crummy old ribbon from the time she won the Viola Swamp Look-Alike Contest in first grade.

"Mom?" Judy asked. "Did you ever get your picture in the paper?"

"Sure," said Mom. "Lots of times. For the high school glee club."

"What's *glee*?" asked Stink.

"*Glee* means being happy," Mom told him, "or cheerful."

"They put your picture in the paper just for being happy?" asked Judy.

"No." Mom laughed. "Glee club is a singing group." Judy did not think anybody would take *her* picture just for being happy.

Or for singing songs about it.

"How about you, Dad?" asked Judy.

"They said my name on the radio once for having the right answer to a quiz-show question."

"What was the question?" asked Stink.

"How many presidents were born in Virginia?"

"How many?" asked Stink and Judy.

"Eight."

"Wow," said Judy.

"Aren't you going to ask me?" asked Stink.

"You never had your picture in the paper," said Judy.

"Yes, I did, didn't I, Mom?" Stink asked. "It's in my baby scrapbook."

"You've heard that story, Judy, about how we waited too long to leave for the hospital and your brother was born in the back of the Jeep."

"I was even on TV! On the news!"

"Oh, yeah," said Judy. "Thanks for reminding me."

It wasn't fair. Her own stinky brother got to be on the real live news. She, Judy Moody, was not even famous enough for the refrigerator.

Infamous

Rocky was already waiting for them at the manhole.

"Hey, Rock," said Stink, "did you ever get your picture in the paper?"

"Sure," said Rocky. "Bunches of times."

"You did?" asked Judy.

"No, not really," said Rocky. "But they did hang my picture up in the library one time."

"See?" Judy said to Stink. "Even my best friend is famous."

"Why'd they hang your picture up in the library?" asked Stink.

"My mom took me to the library to see this magician guy, you know? He did this trick where he took my Superman ring and made it disappear. Then he pulled it out of his sleeve along with a bunch of scarves. They took a picture of it and I'm the kid in the front row with my eyes bugging out. Not exactly famous."

"Still," said Judy.

When Judy got to school, Mr. Todd said, "Let's go over our spelling words." Spelling, spelling, spelling. The whole wide world was hung up on spelling.

Judy leaned over and whispered to Frank. "Hey, Frank, ever had your picture in the paper?"

"It's no big deal," said Frank. "I was three years old."

Adam stood up and spelled the word, "R-E-C-Y-C-L-E."

"What was it for?" whispered Judy.

Hailey stood up and spelled the word, "I-C-I-C-L-E."

"I won the Grandpa Grape Coloring Contest in the newspaper. You had to color this dancing grape cartoon guy. He used to be on grape juice. I couldn't even stay in the lines."

Randi stood up and spelled, "M-O-T-O-R-C-Y-C-L-E."

Even Frank Pearl was famous. For scribbling on a dancing grape.

"Everybody I know is F-A-M-O-U-S," Judy grumped.

"Judy," said Mr. Todd, "were you hoping to get a white card today?"

A white card! Three white cards in one

week meant you had to stay after school! She already had two. And it was only Wednesday.

"Why don't you spell the bonus word aloud for us?" Mr. Todd said.

Bonus word? thought Judy. She hadn't been paying attention. She, Judy Moody, was in a pickle. Pickle? Was that the word? "Could I have the definition please?" she asked.

The whole class cracked up. "It's something you eat," said Rocky.

Judy stood up. "P-O-P-S-I-C-L-E. *Popsicle,*" she announced confidently.

"Very good," said Mr. Todd. "For *popsicle.* Unfortunately that wasn't our bonus spelling word for today."

"Jessica? Would you like to spell the word for the class?"

Jessica Finch stood up tall, holding her pointy head so she looked very queenly. "P-U-M-P-E-R-N-I-C-K-E-L. *Pumpernickel,*" said Jessica, faster than necessary.

Pumpernickel was one of those artichokey kind of words that only Pinch Face herself could spell. *I bet she can't spell* aardwolf, thought Judy.

"Judy," Mr. Todd said, "if you study your spelling words and pay attention in class, you can avoid getting white cards and we'll both get along famously."

There it was again. *That word.*

It was almost time for Science, her best subject, so it would be easy for Judy to pay attention. She'd sit up straight and raise her hand a bunch, like Jessica Finch.

She, Judy Moody, would *not* get another white card.

🌀   🌀   🌀

Judy studied the squirming worm on her desk up close.

"As you all know," said Mr. Todd, "we've been raising mealworms. Today I'm passing one out for each of you to examine. You can often find mealworms at home. Where do you think you would find them in your house?"

Judy raised her hand.

"They like to eat oatmeal and flour and stuff," she said when Mr. Todd called on her.

"So maybe in your kitchen?"

"Right. Good," said Mr. Todd. "They are actually the larvae of a type of beetle. The flour beetle. Mealworms are nocturnal," said Mr. Todd. "Who can explain what that means?"

Judy's hand shot up again.

"Judy?"

"They sleep in the day and wake up at night," said Judy.

"Fine," said Mr. Todd. "This kind of mealworm is called a *T. molitor*. Everyone take a minute and count how many segments you find on your mealworm. Then write it down in your notebook."

Judy counted thirteen segments, not

including the head. She wrote it in her notebook right away. While she waited for the next question, she let the mealworm climb up her finger. She let it climb up her pencil. Rare! The mealworm perched on her eraser.

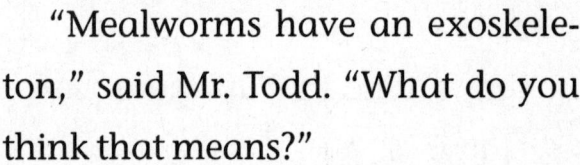

"Mealworms have an exoskeleton," said Mr. Todd. "What do you think that means?"

Judy knew everything about bones and skeletons. Inside ones and out. She knew the answer again. Judy shot her hand straight up in the air. Judy forgot about the pencil in her hand. She forgot about the mealworm on the tip of her eraser.

Mr. Todd called on Rocky.

Judy watched her mealworm fly through the air. She watched it land smack-dab on Jessica Finch. She watched it crawl up the front of Jessica's shirt and right up onto the tip of Jessica's ponytail.

Judy forgot all about the white card. She waved her hand wildly at Jessica until Jessica looked up, then pointed frantically at Jessica's head.

"*Aaagh!*" Jessica screamed worse than a hyena and flicked her hair to shake off the mealworm. *T. molitor* sailed through the air, hit the chalkboard, and fell to the floor. Class 3T went wild.

"Class!" said Mr. Todd, clapping his hands. "Everybody quiet down. Jessica," he

said. "I'll not have anybody throwing mealworms in my classroom." He wrote her name on the board.

"But I didn't... it was... she did!..."

"That's enough. See me after Science for a white card."

Jessica glared squinty-eyed at Judy. Her pointy ears looked pointier. Her pinched-up face looked even pinchier. Judy faced front.

Judy knew it was all her own fault. But she did not want to get a third white card.

Jessica Finch probably never got a white card before, thought Judy. She probably didn't even know before today what it felt like to get in trouble. All Jessica had was one puny little white card, and one puny little white card never hurt anybody.

❀ ❀ ❀

For the rest of the morning, Judy felt more and more like a bug. No, a louse.

After lunch, her neck started to itch. Then her elbow. She scratched her left knee. Her toe itched inside her shoe.

By the end of the day, Judy went to talk to her teacher. "Mr. Todd," she asked, scratching her ankle, "do you think not telling the truth can make a person itch?" *Scratch, scratch, scratch.*

"I think so," said Mr. Todd. "Is there something you're itching to tell me?"

"Yes," said Judy. *Scratch, scratch.* "In Science today?" *Scratch.* "It was my mealworm." *Scratch.* "My fault."

Scratch, scratch. "Not Jessica Finch's."

Judy told the whole truth.

"Thank you," said Mr. Todd. "I appreciate your coming to me with the truth, Judy. I know that's not always easy."

"Does this mean I don't have to get a third white card?"

"I'm afraid not," said Mr. Todd. "I still want you to learn to pay better attention."

Mr. Todd erased Jessica's name on the board and wrote Judy's name in its place. Judy hung her head.

"Honestly, it's not so bad staying after school with me. We'll find something useful to do, okay? Like maybe clean out the fish tank."

"Mr. Todd, is there a word for somebody

who gets famous for all the wrong reasons?" asked Judy.

"Yes," said Mr. Todd. "That would be... *infamous.*"

Fame Is the Pits

Judy peeled a banana.

"Can I have that?" asked Stink. Judy handed him the banana peel.

"Not *that*!" said Stink.

Judy took a monster bite, then handed Stink the banana. She picked up a cherry instead.

"What are you writing?" she asked her dad, popping the cherry into her mouth.

"Garage sale," said Dad. "I'm running an ad in the paper. It's time to get rid of all that old stuff out there."

"Old stuff?" asked Judy, perking up. Old stuff got people in the newspaper. Really really old stuff even got people on TV. "What old stuff?"

"Your old bike, Mom's books from college, Stink's baby clothes."

"Don't we have any old-old stuff?"

"There's Dad," said Stink.

"Thanks a lot," said Dad.

"No. I mean like Cleopatra's eyelash," said Judy. "Or a hammer used to build the Statue of Liberty. You know. Stuff old enough to be really worth something."

"Stuff you didn't know you had and you find out you're rich?" Stink grinned. "Like antiques from your great-great-great-grandmother? You go on TV and they tell you it's worth a bunch of money."

"I'm afraid nobody's going to get rich around here. Our old stuff is junk," said Dad.

"ROAR," said Judy. She pulled the stem off another cherry.

If only she had something unusual. Really rare. Like maybe a broken plate from another century, or an old letter from the American Revolution.

"So, what's happening in school these days?" Dad asked.

Judy sat up. Had Dad heard about the white cards? "What do you mean?"

"I mean, is anything interesting going on?"

"Can I stay after school Friday?" asked Judy. "Mr. Todd says I can help clean the fish tank."

"P-U," said Stink.

"We'll see if Mom can pick you up. How about you, Stink?"

Judy popped another cherry into her mouth.

"We learned this funny story about George Washington," said Stink. "It's about not telling a lie."

Judy chomped down on the cherry.

"See, he chopped down this cherry tree. And when his dad asked who did it, Washington said, 'I cannot tell a lie.' And he told on himself."

Judy almost choked. She spit out her cherry pit. It went zinging across the table at Stink.

"Hey," said Stink. "She spit at me."

"It was an accident," said Judy.

"Judy!" said Dad.

"Okay. Okay. I cannot tell a lie. I coughed a cherry pit at Stink."

"Pick up the cherry pit," said Dad.

Judy reached under Stink's chair and picked it up off the floor.

"No fair," said Judy. "Why should anyone

get famous for telling a lie? The whole story about the lie is a lie!"

"Most people don't realize it's not true," said Dad.

"It's still a good story," said Stink.

Judy turned the cherry pit over and over. It gave her a brilliant Judy-Moody-Gets-Famous idea. A two-hundred-fifty-year-old idea.

Judy took the cherry pit upstairs to her room. She got out her hair dryer, and turned it on HIGH.

"What are you doing?" asked Stink, who had followed her upstairs.

"What does it look like?" said Judy. "I'm blow-drying my cherry pit."

"You're nuts," said Stink.

After he left, Judy got out the tiny hammer from her doctor kit, the one for testing reflexes. She tapped on the cherry pit to give it scars, so it would look old. Very, very old. Next she took a pin and carved the initials GW on the bottom. Then, she took out her clear plastic bug-box, the one with the magnifying glass on top, and put the cherry pit inside for safekeeping, initials-side up.

"Rare!" said Judy. And that was the truth.

֍ ֍ ֍

On the afternoon of the garage sale, Stink had his own table filled with tub toys, rusty Matchbox cars, Lincoln Logs, a rubber band ball, Shrinky Dinks that had already been shrunk, paper cooties, broken rhythm instruments, and glow-in-the-dark bugs he made with his Creepy Crawlers machine.

Matchbox cars   Lincoln Logs   Glow-in-the-dark bugs

"Stink, nobody is going to buy that stuff," Judy told him.

"Yeah, right," said Stink. "And they're going to buy air?" he said, pointing to Judy's empty table.

"You'll see," said Judy. "I have something better than junk." She covered her table with a midnight blue tablecloth that looked like velvet. She put up a sign:

Then she set her magnifying bug-box in the middle of the table. Inside was — *ta da!* — the FAMOUS cherry pit.

Judy added one more line to her sign:

5¢ A LOOK

She could hardly sit still. She wondered how long it would take the newspaper people to come take her picture with the two-hundred-fifty-year-old cherry pit.

Little kids put a nickel in the can and said, "Wow, is that REALLY from George Washington's cherry tree?"

"I cannot tell a lie," said Judy. "It is!"

"Where'd you get it?" they asked.

"It's been in the family forever."

"Forever since last week," said Stink. Judy turned on him with her stinging caterpillar look.

"How do you know it's really George Washington's?" they asked.

"Just look," said Judy. She opened the lid and lifted out the cherry pit. "It says GW right here. See?"

"Let me see," said a girl named Hannah. She showed her little brother. "GW. It's just like M&M's."

"M&M's!" said the boy, and popped the pit into his mouth.

"Ricky, NO!" said his older sister. But it was too late.

"Spit!" said Judy.

"Spit it out, Ricky!" said Hannah.

Ricky gulped!

"Oh, no! Did he swallow it?" asked Judy. "Stick your finger in his mouth. Is it still in there?"

"It's gone," said Hannah. "Say you're sorry, Ricky."

"M&M's. Yum," said Ricky.

"This is the pits," said Judy. "Now what am I going to do when the newspaper comes?"

"Duh. Make another one?" said Stink.

Judy groaned. Judy moaned. In one gulp, that kid had swallowed her famous two-hundred-fifty-year-old George Washington cherry pit. In one gulp, Ricky the neighbor kid had swallowed Judy Moody's ticket to fame.

The only picture of *that* cherry pit would be an x-ray.

Famous Pet Contest

Stink counted his garage sale money at the kitchen table. *Clink. Clink. CLINK.*

"Stink, you're counting that money out loud on purpose," said Judy.

"I can't help it!" said Stink. "Mom, tell her. Money makes noise. When you have so much of it." He grinned.

Judy crumpled up the newspaper that had their garage sale ad in it. She stuffed it angrily into the trash.

"Recycle, please," said Mom.

"Whoa," said Stink. "The recycle queen put paper in the trash?"

"Can I use it to line Mouse's litter box?" asked Judy.

"Good idea," said Mom.

Judy uncrumpled the paper and spread it on the floor to flatten it.

EARLY BIRD SPECIAL! . . .

GARAGE DOOR SALE! . . .

FAMOUS PET CONTEST! . . .

KISS BAD BREATH GOOD-BYE!

Wait! Did that say *famous*? Judy went back and read it again:

> ## FAMOUS PET CONTEST
>
> Bring your pet to
> FUR & FANGS
> this Saturday!
>
> Enter your pet in our
> famous pet-trick contest!
>
> Have fun! Win prizes!
>
> Winners will receive a
> blue ribbon, a gift certificate,
> and get their picture
> published in the
> NORTHERN VIRGINIA STAR!

Judy could not believe her eyes. "Where's Mouse?" she asked. "Upstairs," said Mom.

"Here, Mousey, Mousey," Judy called. Mouse came down the stairs and strolled into the kitchen, looking for some lunch.

Judy scooped up her cat and kissed her on the nose: "*Mww, mww, mwww.* You, the best, most wonderful cat in the whole wide world with tuna fish on top, are going to make *me* famous!"

Visions of blue ribbons and certificates with fancy writing danced in her head. "*And* I get my picture in the paper."

"Hey," she said to her family, "does anybody feel like a piece of toast?"

🌀 🌀 🌀

When Judy hurried into Fur & Fangs with Mouse and Stink that Saturday, it was packed.

Clutching a piece of bread, she said, "Everyone in the entire state of Virginia must own a pet that can do a trick. Hey, there's Frank!"

"And there's Rocky," said Stink.

"You guys! Frank! Rocky! Over here!" Judy called.

Frank's dog, Sparky, sniffed a purple dog bone. Sparky sniffed Judy's ankle. Sparky sniffed a ferret.

"What trick does Sparky do?" Stink asked Frank.

"He jumps through a Hula-Hoop, don't you, boy?" said Frank.

"I brought Houdini," Rocky said, showing them his iguana. "If you scare him, like with a loud noise or something, he can make the end of his tail drop right off."

"Rare," said Judy.

She looked around at all the other pets. There was a rabbit and a turtle, a white rat named Elvis, and a striped salamander.

Judy saw a hamster racing on a wheel, a snake so still it looked fake, and a shell that was supposed to be a hermit crab. Someone had even brought a stuffed monkey.

"Time for the contest!" yelled the pet store lady over all the squeaking and squawking, growling and yowling.

All the people with pets formed a circle. First was a dancing cricket. Then a turtle that rolled over and a rabbit that drank from a straw.

Polly the parrot sang the first five notes of "The Star-Spangled Banner." Judy caught herself clapping.

When it was Frank's turn, Sparky jumped through the Hula-Hoop three times and everybody clapped. Then Rocky could not get Houdini's tail to drop off. "Dogs make him nervous," Rocky explained.

Three pet tricks later, Polly was still singing.

Emily from school had a ferret named Suzy who brushed its own teeth. Stink liked it the best.

"But all it did was eat the toothpaste," said Judy.

When it was Judy's turn, she set up a toaster on the floor, dropped a piece of bread into the slot, then took Mouse out of her cat carrier.

"This is Mouse," Judy told the audience. "She's going to make toast." The audience clapped. Judy stood Mouse on the table. "Don't be nervous," she whispered.

Mouse sat down and began licking her paw.

"Look at the toaster, Mouse," whispered Judy. "The toaster!" Judy pushed it toward Mouse.

Mouse swatted the toaster. Mouse swiped at the toaster. Mouse pushed the toaster away with her paw. Everybody cracked up. Judy held out a Tasty Tuna Treat. Mouse stood up. Mouse saw herself in the toaster!

Judy held her breath.

Mouse swiped at the toaster one more time. This time she pressed down the button with her paw. The slice of bread disappeared! The red coils heated up.

The crowd got quiet. A minute later, the toast popped up.

"Ta da!" called Judy.

"Hooray!" Everybody clapped and cheered.

"Mouse, I'll be famous at last!" Judy squeezed her.

"And now, last but not least," said the pet store lady, "a chicken that plays the piano."

Up stepped David, a boy with a chicken on a leash.

"This is Mozart," said the boy. Mozart pecked out three notes on the toy piano with his beak. "'Three Blind Mice!'" someone yelled. The crowd went wild.

Judy felt a familiar twinge, the tug of a bad mood. She, Judy Moody, would never be as famous as a piano-playing chicken.

For the grand finale, everyone paraded their pets, marching in a circle.

"What a great contest this year," said the pet store lady. "I'd like to thank all of you for coming. Now, for the prizes," said the pet store lady. "If I call your pet's name, please step into the center of the circle."

A man stepped up to the circle with a big camera.

"The newspaper! They're here," Judy announced.

"In third place, Suzy Chang, the toothbrushing ferret."

Please-please-please, Judy wished silently.

"Second place is Mouse Moody, the cat who makes toast!"

"That's you!" said Frank and Rocky, pushing Judy into the circle.

"Mouse, we won!" cried Judy. "Second place!" At last her time had come. At last her chance to be famous.

"And first prize goes to Mozart Puckett, the piano-playing chicken! Let's hear it for all the famous pets!"

The crowd went wild. Each pet got a blue ribbon to wear and a gift certificate to Fur & Fangs. The winners lined up to have a picture taken! Judy was on the end, holding Mouse, but Mouse squirmed and leaped out of Judy's arms. Flash! Judy blinked. The newspaper man snapped a picture faster than lightning.

"Thank you, everybody! That's it!" yelled the pet store lady.

"That's it?" asked Judy.

Judy's fifteen minutes of fame lasted only fifteen seconds. Fifteen seconds of fame, and she, Judy Moody, had blinked.

❧ ❧ ❧

The following morning, Judy ran outside to fetch the paper. She whipped through the pages. Her heart beat faster.

"Here it is!" Judy cried. She could not believe her eyes. There were David Puckett and Emily Chang with mile-wide smiles. There were Mozart the chicken and Suzy the ferret.

"Let me see!" said Stink. "Hey, there's Mouse!"

"I'm not even in the picture!" yelled Judy.

"There you are!" said Stink, pointing to an elbow.

"I'm not famous!" Judy wailed. "I'm an elbow!"

"Let's see," said Dad. He read the caption. "Blah-blah, *winners of the Famous Pet Contest,* blah-blah. It says your name, right here. See? *Mouse and Judy . . . Muddy.*"

"WHAT!" said Judy. "*Muddy*? Let me see."

"Judy Muddy! That's a good one," said Stink.

"Judy Muddy! No one will ever know it's me," said Judy.

"We'll know," said Dad.

Judy frowned. "I guess your name is Mud," Dad said, laughing.

"ROAR!" said Judy.

"At least it says Mouse won the contest," Mom said. She cut out the picture and hung it up on the fridge.

"Great," said Judy. "Even my cat's in the Moody Hall of Fame."

Mom kissed the top of Judy's head. "And you have one very famous elbow."

Broken Records

Judy studied her famous elbow in the mirror. She squished her elbow into a wrinkled happy face. She squinched her elbow into a mad face.

If Judy ever hoped to be more famous than an elbow, she needed some help. Judy called all members of the Toad Pee Club. "Meet at the clubhouse," she told everybody.

Rocky, Frank, and Judy crowded into the blue tent in her backyard. Last was Stink, who carried Toady, their mascot, in one hand, and walked while reading a book.

"Stink, you better watch out or you'll renew your membership."

"OH!" said Stink. He tossed Toady into the bucket before the toad famous for peeing in people's hands did it again.

"Now," said Judy, "how can we make me famous?"

"Let's think," Rocky said.

"Stink, you're not thinking," said Judy.

"Getting famous is boring," said Stink, leafing through his book.

"Stink, what book could be sooooooooooo interesting?"

Stink held up the *Guinness Book of World Records*. Judy looked at Frank. Frank looked at Rocky. Rocky looked at Judy. "Brainstorm!" the three yelled at the same time. Then they cracked up.

"Stink, you are a genius. The secret to getting famous is right there in your hands."

Stink checked his hands.

"Don't you get it?" said Judy. "I could break a record and get in that book! Then I'd be superfamous."

"Famous. Famous. Famous. YOU are a broken record," Stink told her.

"Hardee-har-har," said Judy.

"You know how you collect stuff, like

Band-Aids?" said Frank. "You could break a record for collecting something. Like the most pizza tables."

"Or scabs!" said Judy.

"*Bluck*," said Stink. "There's a guy in here who collects throw-up bags from airplanes. He has two thousand one hundred and twelve. One bag even has a connect-the-dots drawing of Benjamin Franklin on it."

"That's way better than scabs," said Judy.

"Hey, look," Rocky said, reading over Stink's shoulder. "World's longest word. Spell that and you could be the next Jessica Finch."

The word was: *Pneumonoultramicroscopicsilicovolcanoconiosis.*

"Whoa. Forty-five letters," said Frank, counting.

"Not even Queen Bee herself could spell that!" said Judy.

"It says here it's an ucky disease from volcanoes," Rocky said. "No lie."

"Wait! I got it. There's a guy in here with the longest neck," said Stink. "We could all pull on your head to stretch your neck out!"

"I want to be famous, not a giraffe," said Judy.

"With a giraffe neck you would be famous," Stink told her.

"Let me see that book." Judy grabbed the book of records and flipped through the pages. Longest gum wrapper chain? It took thirty-one years to make! Longest fingernail? No way; the guy hasn't cut his thumbnail since 1952. Best spitter? Judy could spit.

Then she saw it. Right there on page 399.

The human centipede!

"Okay. Listen up. We're going to be a giant creepy-crawly," said Judy. "Let's tie our shoelaces together, then walk like a caterpillar. The old record is ninety-eight feet and five inches. Rocky, remember last summer we measured with a string? It was one hundred feet to your house and back. So all we have to do is walk from here to Rocky's and back to break the record."

They sat in a line, one behind the other,

like desks in a row. First Judy, then Frank, Rocky, and Stink.

"Hey, I'm always last!" said Stink.

"You're the rear end," said Judy.

"Tie one shoelace to the person in front, and one to the person in back," she called.

"How are we ever going to stand up?" asked Stink.

"On the count of three," Judy began. "One, two . . ." Judy took the first step. Frank's foot shot up and out from under him. Like bowling pins, Frank toppled sideways, Rocky fell over on his ear, and Stink crashed on his elbows.

Frank snorted first. Rocky cracked up so bad he sprayed everybody.

"Hic-CUP!" said Stink.

When they were finally standing, without anybody falling or snorting or hiccupping, they each tried to take a step. One . . . two . . . three.

"The human centipede!" called Judy. She pictured the human centipede in her imagination—growing longer and longer, all wiggly and squiggly with tons of legs, and she, Judy Moody, at the head with biting fangs and poison claws!

"*Hssss!*" said Judy.

"No hopping, Rocky," called Frank.

"My lace is all twisted," said Rocky.

"Hold up!" yelled Stink from the end of the line.

That's when it happened.

Judy stopped, but the rest of the centipede kept going! They all began to fall. *Crunch!* Judy stepped on Frank's hand. Frank's other arm socked Rocky in the stomach. Stink's foot landed in Rocky's hair.

Three steps, and they had crumbled into a human pretzel.

"Hey! Watch it!" Stink yelled.

"I'm all twisted," Rocky said.

"OWWWWWWWWWWWW!" Frank screamed. Frank was holding up his right arm with his left hand.

Frank Pearl's right pinky finger looked all floppy. It looked all floopy. Frank Pearl's pinky was twice as fat as normal and dangled down the wrong way.

"OOOH! What happened?" asked Judy.

"It hurts . . . bad," said Frank, tears streaming down his face. "Real bad."

"Stink, run and get Mom. Fast!"

What if Judy had broken a finger, not a record? If Frank's pinky was broken, it was all Judy's fault.

Judy no longer felt like a human centipede. She, Judy Moody, felt more like a human *worm*.

Broken Parts

"So which one of you's the patient?" asked a tall man with a red beard in a long white coat.

Frank held up his little blue sausage of a finger.

"Ouch!" said the man. "How'd this happen?"

Frank looked over at Judy. Judy stared a hole in the carpet.

"We were playing," Frank answered.

"We were making a human centipede so my sister could be famous!" said Stink. "And she stepped on Frank!"

Judy sent Stink her best troll-eyes stare, complete with stinging-caterpillar eyebrows. The man laughed. "Okay. Well. I'm Ron, the emergency-room nurse. I'll take you back, and the doctor's gonna fix you right up, Frank. Is your mom or dad here?"

"My mom went to call Frank's mom," said Judy.

"Okay. Tell you what. The children's wing is right through those red doors. Why don't you two wait in the playroom there. It'll be more fun. I'll tell your mom you're there, when she comes back."

Too bad Rocky went home. Now she was

stuck with Stink. They pushed through the red doors and into a long hallway. At the end of the hall was a room marked THE MAGIC PLAYROOM. Judy and Stink went in.

The walls were papered with teddy bears in hospital gowns, holding balloons. Each bear had crutches or bandages or sat in a wheelchair. There was a couch, a table with crayons and paper for coloring, a plastic castle, and a bookshelf with books about going to the hospital. There was even a miniature operating table on wheels. The only kid in the playroom was a girl in a wheelchair.

"How come you're in a wheelchair?" Stink asked her.

"Stink, you shouldn't ask stuff like that."

"It's okay," said the girl. "I got a new heart. They can't let me walk around yet. They have to keep me at the hospital for a long, long time to make sure it works."

"A whole new heart! Wow!" said Stink. "What's wrong with your old one?"

"Stink!" said Judy, even though she wanted to know too.

"It broke, I guess," said the girl.

"Were you scared?" Judy asked.

The girl nodded. "Guess what. My scar goes from my neck all the way down to my bellybutton."

"What's your name?" asked Stink.

"Laura," said the girl.

"That's one brave heart you got there, Laura," said Judy.

"Daddy says I'm a brave girl," Laura said. "I'm getting a hamster when I go home. Do you have a hamster?"

"No," said Judy. "I have a cat named Mouse."

"There's nothing to do here," said Laura, looking around.

"They have doctor stuff," said Judy.

"Look! A real sling and stuff!" said Stink, kneeling next to a big cardboard box. He pulled out Ace bandages, boxes of gauze, and tongue depressors. Even a stethoscope and a pair of crutches.

"Stink, can I put your arm in a sling?" Judy asked.

"No way," said Stink.

"How about you, Laura? I know how. For real."

"I'm sick of doctor stuff," Laura said.

"What about dolls?" Stink asked. "There's a bunch of dolls in this box."

"They all have broken arms and legs, or no heads," Laura said. "And some of them have cancer."

"What do you mean?" Judy asked.

"They're bald, like Sarah, in my same room."

"That's not fair," Judy said. "They should at least have dolls to play with that aren't sick."

The nurse came back just then. "Time to go back to your room," she told Laura. "Did you kids meet our brave girl?"

"Yes!" said Judy and Stink.

"I hope your new heart works great!" said Judy, as Laura left with the nurse.

"Bye!" called Stink.

Judy looked through the doll box. Laura was right. All the dolls were dirty or broken or hairless or headless.

Mrs. Moody poked her head in the doorway. "Hello!"

"Mom!" said Stink.

"Is Frank okay?" Judy asked.

"His finger's broken," said Mrs. Moody, "but his mom is with him now. He's getting a splint."

"Rare! A real splint!" said Judy.

"He won't be playing any basketball for a while, but he's going to be just fine. So. Ready to go?"

Stink and Judy followed Mrs. Moody out of the playroom. Halfway down the hall, Judy stopped, holding Stink back by his shirt.

"Stink," she said so her mom couldn't hear. "Give me your backpack."

"What?"

"Your backpack. I need it." Stink made a face and handed over the pack.

"Catch up with Mom and tell her I forgot something. I'll be right back."

Judy dashed back into the playroom and over to the box of broken dolls. Looking around to make sure no one was coming, she stuffed the dolls into the backpack. Judy zipped it shut, flung it over her shoulder like a lumpy Santa Claus sack, and headed back down the hall.

When Mom stopped to ask a question at the desk, Stink asked, "Hey! What's in there?"

"Nothing."

"Nothing does not make a big fat lump.

Did you take that doctor stuff? You took stuff! You stole! I'm telling!"

"Shh! You can't tell anybody, Stink, or we'll get in trouble for stealing."

"We? You mean *you'll* get in trouble," said Stink. "Are you crazy? Do you want to be famous for being the only third grader who ever went to jail?"

"Swear you won't tell, Stink."

"What will you give me?"

"I'll let you look at real spit under my microscope."

"Okay. I swear."

"You swore!" said Judy. "I'm telling."

Body Parts

As soon as Judy got home, she unloaded the backpack and spread the dolls out on her bottom bunk. She, Doctor Judy Moody, was in an operating mood. On her bed was a doll that didn't talk or cry anymore, and one with no arms. There was a headless doll, and one that was bald.

First Judy gave each of the dolls a bath.

"I know just what I need," said Judy.

"Body parts!" She dug out her collection: long arms, skinny arms, brown legs, pink legs, middles with bellybuttons, one bare foot, a thing that looked like a neck, and all sorts of heads—small heads, fat heads, Barbie heads, bald heads! Judy emptied a whole bag of body parts onto her bed. "Rare!"

Judy glued a red wig with yarn braids onto the doll with no hair and gave another one arms that bent. Judy bent the arm back and forth, back and forth, to test it out. "Boo!" said the doll each time Judy lifted her arm.

"You don't scare me!" Judy told the doll.

"And for you," she said to the headless

doll. "A new head!" From all the heads on her bed, Judy chose one with brown hair and green eyes.

"There you go," said Judy, popping on the new head. But when she turned the doll upside down to put some shoes on her, the doll's head flew off and bounced across the floor!

"Whoa!" said Judy, running after the head. "That won't work. Let's try this one. How would you like eyes that can close and open?" Judy twisted the new head onto the doll's neck and waved her up, down, up, down through the air a few times to watch the eyes open and close.

"Voilà!" said Judy. She kissed the doll right on the nose.

Next she dressed each doll in a blue-and-white hospital gown she made from an old sheet, and gave each of them a paper bracelet printed with a name: Colby, Molly, Suzanna, Laura.

"Knock, knock," called Stink, pounding on her door.

"Go away," said Judy.

"Knock, knock!" said Stink.

"Who's there?" said Judy.

"I, Stink," said Stink.

"I Stink who?"

"I stink you should let me in your room," said Stink, letting himself in anyway. He peeked behind the blanket hanging over the bottom bunk.

"*Aaagh!*" he yelled, jumping back in shock. "Those dolls! The hospital—you stole! Those are . . . those aren't . . . if Mom and Dad find out . . ."

"Stink, you *promised* you wouldn't tell."

"Yeah, but . . ."

Judy was making a tiny cast out of oogey

wet newspaper. "Look, if you keep quiet, I'll let you help me."

"It's a deal!" said Stink.

Stink and Judy finished putting the cast on one of the doll's legs. When it dried, they painted it white and signed it with lots of made-up names. After that, they made a sling for another doll, with a scrap of cloth. On a different doll Doctor Judy put tattoo Band-Aids from her Band-Aid collection all over its legs, arms, and stomach.

"Double cool!" said Stink.

Last but not least was a rag doll made of cloth. Judy took a pink marker and drew a scar from the doll's neck down to her belly-button. Then she drew a red heart, broken in two. With black thread, she stitched the broken heart back together, hiding it under the doll's hospital gown.

"Just like that girl Laura!" Stink said.

When she was finished, Judy propped up all the dolls in a row on her bottom bunk and stood back to admire her work. She set her own doll, Hedda-Get-Betta, next to them.

"Wow, you made them look really good!" said Stink.

A little later Judy packed all the dolls into a box and secretly mailed them back to the hospital. Without a return address, no one would ever know that she was the one who had stolen the dolls.

It's like a real doll hospital, thought Judy. She, Judy Moody, was on her way to being just like First Woman Doctor, Elizabeth Blackwell.

Judy Moody and Jessica Flinch

On Monday morning Mr. Todd asked, "Where's Frank today?"

"Absent," said Judy.

"Oh, that's right. I heard that he broke his finger. Does anybody know how it happened?"

"It's a loooooooooooooooooooong story," said Judy.

"As long as a centipede!" said Rocky.

"I heard Judy Moody stepped on him!"

said Adam. "CRACK!" He bent his finger back like it was breaking.

"Okay, okay. We'll ask Frank all about it when he gets back."

"He'll be back tomorrow," Judy said.

Judy looked at the empty desk next to her. Without Frank, there was no one to snort at her jokes. Without Frank, she spelled *barnacle* with an *i*. Without Frank, she had nobody to tease about eating paste.

To make matters worse, all morning Jessica Finch kept inching her desk a little closer, a little closer to Judy.

"Is that the elbow that was in the paper?" Jessica asked.

Judy drew a mad face on her famous elbow and pointed it at Jessica.

"Hey, Judy? Want to come over to my house after school?" asked Jessica. "I could show you my glow-in-the-dark spelling posters."

"Can't," said Judy.

"Why not?"

"I have to feed Jaws, my Venus flytrap."

"How about tomorrow?"

"I feed it every day," said Judy.

"How about after you feed Jaws?" asked Jessica.

"Homework," said Judy.

The truth: by Friday Judy was almost bored enough to go to Jessica's. Rocky had to stay at his grandma's after school for a week because his mom was working late, and Frank could hardly do anything with a broken finger.

Too bad she had finished operating on all the hospital dolls so quickly. Making a cast was the best!

If only she could try making a bigger cast, on a human patient. But who? Stink would not let her near him with wet oogey newspaper.

Judy looked back at Jessica Finch. Maybe she did not look like a Pinch Face. Maybe she did not look like an aardwolf. Maybe she looked like . . . a doctor's dream. The perfect patient!

"Hey, Jessica," Judy asked, "how would you like to get your arm in a cast?"

"It's not broken," Jessica said.

"Who cares?" said Judy. "It's just for fun."

"Sure, I guess. Does this mean you'll come over? I can show you my spelling posters."

"How does today after school sound?" asked Judy.

When Judy got to Jessica Finch's house, the two girls went up to Jessica's room. Judy looked around. All she could see were pigs. Pink pigs. Stuffed pigs. Piggy banks. A fuzzy piggy-face rug. Even Jessica's bed looked like a pig wearing a pink skirt.

"You like pigs!" said Judy.

"What was your first clue?" Jessica laughed in her hyena way.

Judy touched the spelling bee prize ribbons Jessica had hanging on the wall. Jessica showed Judy her scrapbook, with all the times her name had been in the paper.

"Wow," said Judy. "Did they ever spell your name wrong?"

"Once. Jessica Flinch!"

"Judy Muddy!" said Judy.

"Look! Here are all the spelling posters I made." Jessica pointed to the wall next to her bed.

"Hey, they're green. How come they're not pink too?"

"Because they glow in the dark. Wait." Jessica pulled down the shades and turned off the light.

The room lit up with glow-in-the-dark words. All the spelling words from Mr. Todd!

BICYCLE

ICICLE

BREADSICLE

POPSICLE

RECYCLE

MOTORCYCLE

"What's a breadsicle?" Judy asked. "Is that like pumpernickel?"

"Hey, you're good," said Jessica. "See, I make up fake words and play a game to see if I can fool myself. Want to play? Or we could play the pig game. Instead of dice you get to roll little plastic pigs."

"What about making a cast?" said Judy.

"You're not going to break my finger or anything, like you did to Frank, are you?"

"No! Besides, it was an accident," Judy said.

"Okay. So. What do we need?" asked Jessica.

"Newspaper. Water. Glue."

"This comes off, right?" said Jessica.

"Right," said Judy. *There must be some way to get it off,* she thought. "We have to let it dry first. Then we paint it."

"Can we paint it pink?" asked Jessica.

"Sure," Judy said. *Rare. A pink cast.*

"I'll go get some old newspapers," said Jessica.

When she came back, she said, "All I could find was today's, so let's hope my parents have already read it!"

Judy and Jessica tore the paper into strips. Judy could not wait to see the pink cast. This was her biggest operation yet!

Judy dipped paper strips into the sticky mixture and carefully placed them one by one on Jessica's arm.

"Ooh. It feels icky," said Jessica. "Are you sure this is going to work?"

Jessica was as bad as Stink. "Here," said Judy, handing Jessica more newspaper. "Tear up some more strips. I'm running out."

Jessica handed Judy a strip. At the top was the word PHANTOM. Jessica handed Judy another strip. STRIKES. A third. HOSPITAL.

"Stop!" said Judy. "Where's the rest of this story?" She peered at Jessica's arm. "Page B six. Where's page B six, huh?"

"Oh. I think I already ripped it up."

Judy tried to read Jessica's wet, oogey arm, but all she could make out were the

words *doll thief.* "What did it say?" she asked in a panic.

"Phantom strikes county hospital, or something."

"Or something, what?"

"I don't know. What's the big deal?"

Judy stood up suddenly, scattering paper strips everywhere. "I gotta go!"

"You what? Wait! My arm! You can't just... What about my pink cast?" But Judy was already out the door.

She, Judy Moody, Doll Thief, would be famous all right. For going to jail. Just like Stink said.

Judy Moody, Superhero

"Home already?" asked Mom. "How was Jessica's? Fun?"

"I . . . did you . . . where's . . . the . . . paper?" Judy asked, out of breath.

"Today's paper? Right here," said Dad, pushing it across the table toward Judy.

Judy flipped through the paper madly. But when she got to Section B, all she saw was a giant hole.

"Who cut up the paper? Stink?" she said, shooting him her best stinging-caterpillar eyebrow look.

"Oh, I did," said Dad. "Here, I tacked it up right here on the fridge."

He read out loud:

PHANTOM DOLL DOCTOR STRIKES COUNTY HOSPITAL

On Saturday, October 17, Grace Porter, a member of the nursing staff at County General, noticed that several of the dolls that had been donated to the hospital for its Magic Playroom were missing.

"Funny coincidence," said Mom. "That was the same day we took Frank to the hospital!"

"Ha. Funny," said Judy, trying to smile. Mom would not find it so funny when she learned that her only daughter was an all-out, true-blue, I-before-E thief.

Dad continued reading:

The missing dolls created quite a stir. Young patients who use the Magic Playroom in the Children's Wing spent days speculating as to the identity of the doll thief.

"Isn't that where I found you two?" asked Mom. "The Magic Playroom?" Judy's mother sounded just like a detective. *Jail time.*

> Curiously, a mysterious package was received a few days later, with all the dolls magically cleaned, scrubbed, fixed, or mended. Each one was tagged, dressed in a hospital gown, and had been properly "doctored" with fancy Band-Aids, slings, and casts.

Dad paused and said, "Hmm. Band-Aids." *Uh-oh,* thought Judy. *Evidence.*

> A special doll with a once-broken heart was given to patient Laura Chumsky, who recently underwent the hospital's twenty-ninth heart transplant. On behalf of Laura Chumsky and all the young patients, the hospital staff would like to thank the anonymous donor, the Phantom Doll Doctor, for this kind contribution.

"It sounds like one of the superheroes in my comics!" Stink said.

"That's quite a story," said Dad, grinning.

"Let me see that," Judy said. She had to see it, had to read it, with her very own eyes. "Phantom Doll Doctor," she repeated, touching the words in the headline. "Rare!"

"What a thoughtful thing for someone to do," said Mom.

"Wish I'd thought of it," said Dad, tacking the article back up on the refrigerator with a pineapple magnet. There it was, front and center in the Moody Hall of Fame.

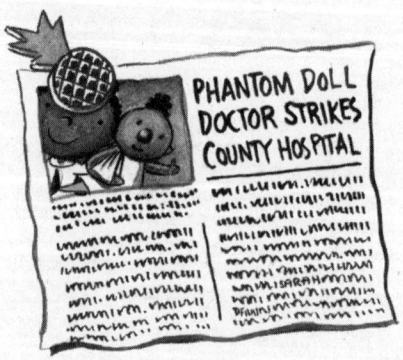

"Too bad," said Stink.

"What's too bad?" said Judy.

"I kind of wanted to see the inside of a jail."

"Hardee-har-har," said Judy, nervously glancing at her parents. But they were both grinning proudly. That's when Judy's brain began working on a brand-new Judy Moody idea.

She'd make a sign. Maybe set up shop in the garage. Get other kids to give her their broken dolls or old stuffed animals. Or she'd find some at yard sales. She would doctor them up and donate them to more sick kids in the Children's Wing at the hospital. Some could have Ace bandages, or fancy scars, or tubes for breathing. Maybe even an IV!

And it could all be in secret. The hospital would never know the identity of the Phantom Doll Doctor. The way nobody knew Superman was really Clark Kent, a nice, quiet reporter from the *Daily Planet*.

Rare!

For the first time in a long time, the once Judy Muddy felt more famous than an elbow.

She, Judy Moody, Phantom Doll Doctor, now felt as famous as Queen Elizabeth, as famous as George Washington, as famous as Superman.

Famouser!

Wouldn't Elizabeth Blackwell, First Woman Doctor, be proud!

Megan McDonald

is the award-winning author of the Judy Moody series. She says that most of Judy's stories "grew out of anecdotes about growing up with my four sisters." She confesses, "I *am* Judy Moody. Same-same! In my family of sisters, we're famous for exaggeration. Judy Moody is me . . . exaggerated." Megan McDonald lives with her husband in northern California.

Peter H. Reynolds

says he felt an immediate connection to Judy Moody because, "having a daughter, I have witnessed firsthand the adventures of a very independent-minded girl." Peter H. Reynolds lives in Massachusetts, just down the street from his twin brother.

Praise for Judy Moody Gets Famous!

An Association of Booksellers for Children
Children's Choice

An American Library Association Notable Children's Book

An International Reading Association Children's Choice

A *Children's Literature* Choice List Title

An Oppenheim Toy Portfolio Gold Award Winner

A Sasquatch Reading Award Nominee (Washington)

"Everything about these Judy Moody books spells G-O-O-D N-E-W-S for early chapter-book readers."
— *The Horn Book*

★ "Even Judy could spell two words that describe both the plot and its heroine: F-R-E-S-H and F-U-N-N-Y."
— *Publishers Weekly* (starred review)

"A disarming plot and likable characters are matched to an equally appealing format." — *Kirkus Reviews*

Be sure to read Judy's next adventure!

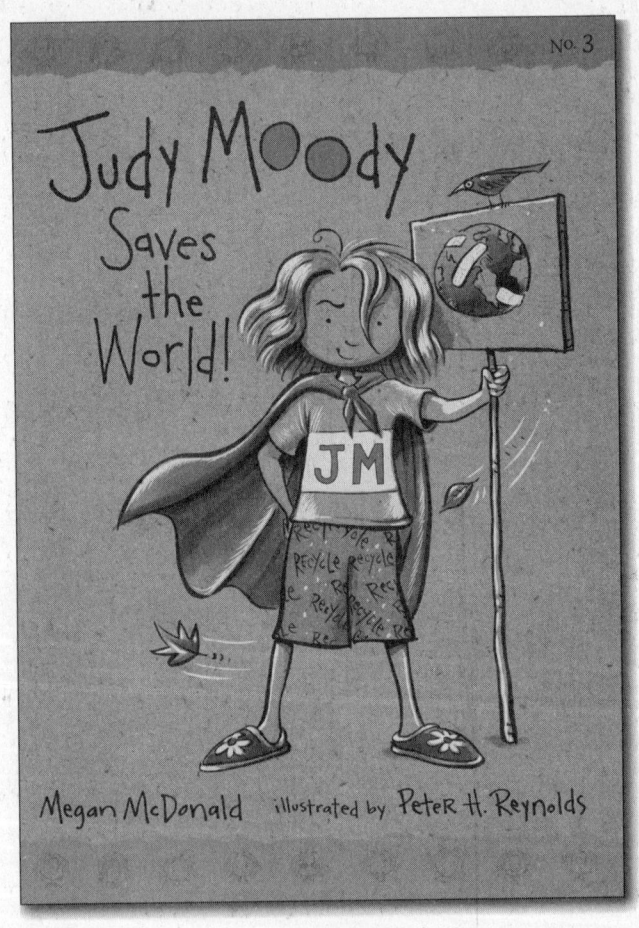

DOUBLE RARE!
Judy Moody has her own website!

Come visit **www.judymoody.com**
for the latest in all things Judy Moody, including:

- All you need to know about the best-ever Judy Moody Fan Club

- Answers to all your V.I.Q.s (very important questions) about Judy

- Way-not-boring stuff about Megan McDonald and Peter H. Reynolds

- Double-cool activities that will be sure to put you in a mood — and not a bad mood, a good mood!

- Totally awesome T.P. Club info!

Look out, Judy Moody!

Stink

is starring in his very own series!

Be sure to check out Stink's adventures!

Experience all of Judy Moody's moods!

Judy Moody Saves the World!

Books by Megan McDonald and Peter H. Reynolds:
    #1 – *Judy Moody*
    #2 – *Judy Moody Gets Famous!*
    #3 – *Judy Moody Saves the World!*
    #4 – *Judy Moody Predicts the Future*
    #5 – *Judy Moody, M.D.: The Doctor Is In!*
    #6 – *Judy Moody Declares Independence*
    #7 – *Judy Moody Around the World in 8½ Days*
    #1 – *Stink: The Incredible Shrinking Kid*
    #2 – *Stink and the Incredible Super-Galactic Jawbreaker*
    #3 – *Stink and the World's Worst Super-Stinky Sneakers*
    Judy Moody and Stink: The Holly Joliday
    The Judy Moody Mood Journal
Judy Moody's Double-Rare Way-Not-Boring Book of Fun Stuff to Do

Books by Megan McDonald:
Ant and Honey Bee: What a Pair!
The Sisters Club

Books by Peter H. Reynolds:
The Dot
Ish
So Few of Me

Judy Moody Saves the World!

Megan McDonald

illustrated by
Peter H. Reynolds

CANDLEWICK PRESS
CAMBRIDGE, MASSACHUSETTS

Text copyright © 2002 by Megan McDonald
Illustrations copyright © 2002 by Peter H. Reynolds
Judy Moody font copyright © 2004 by Peter H. Reynolds

Judy Moody®. Judy Moody is a registered trademark
of Candlewick Press, Inc.

All rights reserved. No part of this book may be reproduced,
transmitted, or stored in an information retrieval system in any form
or by any means, graphic, electronic, or mechanical, including
photocopying, taping, and recording, without prior written
permission from the publisher.

First paperback edition in this format 2006

The Library of Congress has cataloged the hardcover edition as follows:

McDonald, Megan.
Judy Moody saves the world! / Megan McDonald ;
illustrated by Peter H. Reynolds. —1st ed.
p. cm.
Summary: When Judy Moody gets serious about protecting the
environment, her little brother, Stink, thinks she is
overdoing it, but she manages to inspire her third-grade class to
undertake an award-winning, environment-saving project.
ISBN 978-0-7636-1446-1 (hardcover)
[1. Environmental protection— Fiction. 2. Brothers and sisters—Fiction.
3. Schools—Fiction. 4. Contests—Fiction. 5. Virginia—Fiction.
6. Humorous stories.]   I. Reynolds, Peter, ill. II. Title.
PZ7.M1487 Ju 2002
[Fic]—dc21   2001025884

ISBN 978-0-7636-2087-5 (paperback)

10

Printed in the United States of America

This book was typeset in Stone Informal.
The illustrations were done in watercolor, tea, and ink.

Candlewick Press
2067 Massachusetts Avenue
Cambridge, Massachusetts 02140

visit us at www.candlewick.com

for Richard
— M. M.

for all the librarians who believe a good story can save the world!
— P. H. R.

Table of Contents

Crazy Strips Contest 1
Batty for Banana Peels 15
A Mr. Rubbish Mood 26
Pigtoes, Pumas, and Pimplebacks . . 42
Beetle Emergency 55
Pond Scum 64
Luna Two 78
Batty for Band-Aids 95
Project P.E.N.C.I.L. 107
Batty for Bottles 122
The Winking Disease 128

Who's

Judy

The heroine and garbologist, famous for her many moods.

Dad

Judy's father. Has a taste for rain forest coffee beans.

Mom

Judy's mother. Needs a lesson in recycling.

Mouse

Judy's cat. Fond of bananas.

Stink

Judy's younger brother. Batty about bats and Toady.

Who

Toady

Endangered
T. P. Club mascot.

Rocky

Judy's best friend since
FOREVER. Hot on the
trail of the Shenandoah
salamander.

Mr. Todd

Judy's teacher.
Leader of the 3T
ecosystem.

Frank

Judy's stamp-collecting friend.
Knows a thing or two about
monkeyface mussels.

Jessica

Judy's classmate.
Pig fanatic and
pencil freak.

Crazy Strips Contest

Judy Moody did not set out to save the world. She set out to win a contest. A Band-Aid contest.

Judy snapped open her doctor kit. Where was that box of Crazy Strips? She lifted out the tiny hammer for testing reflexes.

"Hey, can I try that?" asked Stink, coming into Judy's room.

"Stink, didn't you ever hear of going knock, knock?"

"Sure," said Stink. "Who's there?"

"Not the joke," said Judy. "The thing a little brother is supposed to do before entering a big sister's room."

"You mean I have to tell a joke just to come in your room?" asked Stink.

"Never mind," said Judy.

"Never mind who?" asked Stink.

"Stink! Just sit on the bed and cross your legs," said Judy. "I'm going to test your reflexes."

"Please don't do doctor stuff to me!" Stink said.

"C'mon, Stink." Judy tapped Stink's knee with the hammer. Stink's foot shot out and kicked her in the leg.

"Hey, Stink," said Judy. "You kicked me!

Who do you think you are, a cassowary?"

"A what-o-wary?"

"Cass-o-wary. I learned it in Science. It's a rain forest bird that can't fly, so it kicks its enemies."

"I'm not a casso-whatever," said Stink. "I just have really good reflexes."

Judy flashed her best anaconda eyes at Stink. "Forget it," she said, putting the hammer away.

Stink reached into Judy's doctor kit and pulled out some Crazy Strips.

"Stink! I told you not to steal my Crazy Strips. Now this box is empty, as in ALL GONE. I told you I'd put your arm in a sling if you didn't stop stealing my stuff."

Stink did not want his arm in a sling

again. Especially when it wasn't broken. "Give it," said Judy, taking the box from Stink. "I want to read about the contest."

"Contest?" asked Stink. "What do we have to do?"

Judy read the box.

Crazy Strips 5th Annual
Design Your Own Bandage Contest.

Create your own Crazy Strip.
Draw with pencils, crayons,
or markers.
Think of a theme.
Go wild with a style.
Be outrageous. Be you.

"You mean we draw something to go on a Crazy Strip?" asked Stink. "What do we win?"

Judy read on.

> Thirteen top designs will be chosen to be printed on Crazy Strips. Just think — kids all across the country could be wearing YOUR creative, colorful Crazy Strip.

"Is that all?" asked Stink.

"Rare!" Judy said. "I, Judy Moody, could have my own Crazy Strip."

"They have to let you win something," Stink said, grabbing the box from Judy.

"Just think. Knees, ankles, and elbows everywhere will be wearing a Judy Moody original. Even Elizabeth Blackwell, First Woman Doctor, didn't have her own Crazy Strip."

"Oh, brother," said Stink. "Before you get too famous, can I use some of your skinny markers?"

"What for?" Judy asked.

"I want to draw a Crazy Strip, too. It says here the Grand Prize is a pair of Rollerblades."

"Rollerblades! Let me see that."

Top Winner: Crazy Strip of the Year
Rollerblades plus your design printed on a Crazy Strip for one year

Runners-up: Crazy Strip of the Month
Crazy Strips sunglasses plus your design printed on a Crazy Strip for one month

All participants receive Honorable Mention certificates.

"Dream on, Stink. Only one kid in the whole entire United States of America gets Rollerblades."

"So?"

"So look at some of the kids who won last year. They're ten years old. Eleven. One is even thirteen. That's a teenager. You're only seven."

"And a quarter," said Stink.

"You'd have to be Picasso for them to pick your design," she said.

"Who?"

"You know. The guy who painted all those blue people."

"Then let me borrow your blue marker," said Stink.

Judy dumped all the markers, crayons,

colored pencils, and pastels she had on the floor. Stink grabbed the first blue marker he saw and started to draw.

"What are you drawing?"

"Bats," said Stink. "Blue bats."

"*You're* bats," said Judy. "People don't like bats."

"But bats eat millions of insects," said Stink. "People should like bats."

"I know *that*," said Judy. "I'm just saying, bats are not going to beat a teenager." Stink kept right on coloring bats.

"Your bats sure have big ears," said Judy.

"They're Virginia big-eared bats."

"Oh," said Judy.

Stink was a good artist, but Judy didn't

want him thinking he was a genius or anything. She had to dream up a good-as-Picasso idea. Better than ucky old bats. Better than a teenager. She wanted her Judy Moody Crazy Strip to be seen all across the U.S.A. The world. The universe.

"Stink, stop squeaking," said Judy.

"It's the magic markers."

"I can't think with all that squeaking," Judy said.

Judy studied some of the other winners on the box from last year. There were ladybugs, flowers, soccer balls, rainbows, and peace signs. Happy, happy, happy. Judy tried to think of something happy to draw on her Crazy Strip.

She drew smiley faces. Yellow, red, blue, green, and purple smiley faces. Underneath she wrote CRAZY STRIPS CURE BAD MOODS.

"Everybody draws smiley faces," said Stink.

"Who?" asked Judy.

"Heather Strong, in my class. And teenagers."

Stink was right. Smiley faces were not good enough to decorate the ankles of millions. Smiley faces were not good enough to win Rollerblades. Smiley faces were not Picasso.

Judy turned her Crazy Strip upside down. The smiley faces turned into bad-mood faces.

"Nobody wants a cranky Crazy Strip," Stink said.

"ROAR!" said Judy.

"They like it if you have a message," said Stink, "but I can't think of a message about bats."

"How about BATTY FOR BAND-AIDS?"

"That's good!" said Stink. "Thanks!"

Stink was already done with his Crazy Strip and Judy still did not have a single idea. Not one inspiration.

"Okay, let's go mail this," said Stink.

Fresh air! That was it! Maybe Judy's brain just needed some good old-fashioned oxygen.

On the way to the mailbox, Stink asked, "Do you think I'll win?"

"What am I? A crystal ball?" asked Judy.

"How long do you think it takes?" asked Stink, dropping the envelope into the big blue box.

"Longer than one second," said Judy.

On the way home, Judy gulped in fresh air.

"You look like a goldfish in a toilet," Stink said.

It was no use. Fresh air was not helping. Fresh air just made her look like a toilet fish.

Stink's Crazy Strip was already in the mail. What if Stink won the contest? What if she could never ever even come up with an idea?

She, Judy Moody, was in a mood.

Batty for Banana Peels

All day Saturday and all day Sunday, Judy could not think up one single creative, award-winning Crazy Strips idea. On Monday morning, as soon as she got to the bus stop, Judy told her best friend, Rocky, about the contest. "Help me think of an idea!"

"I know," said Rocky. "How about a disappearing one? You put it on your arm, only it's clear, so it's invisible."

"Rare!" said Judy. "A disappearing Crazy Strip! That's good!"

"How are you going to win the contest if they can't even see it?" Stink asked.

"Good point," said Judy, thinking it over. "I want the world to be able to *see* my Grand Prize–winning Judy Moody Crazy Strip."

❂   ❂   ❂

At school, Judy was dying to ask Frank Pearl if he had any ideas, but the bell had already rung and she could not risk getting another white card for talking. She already had to stay after school once and clean the fish tank with Mr. Todd for getting three white cards. A person could only clean so many stinky fish tanks.

So she wrote a note about the contest to pass to Frank instead. At the bottom she wrote: *P. S. DON'T let Jessica Finch see this.*

"Science, everybody," said Mr. Todd. "Let's continue our discussion of the environment. Rain forests everywhere are being cut down. When you take medicine or bounce a ball or pop a balloon, you're using something that came from the rain forest. And right here at home, malls are replacing trees, animals are disappearing, and we're running out of places to put all of our trash.

"Today, let's come up with ways we can help save the earth. Sometimes it's good to start small. Think of ways we can help at home. In our own families. And at school. Any ideas?"

"Don't leave lights on," said Hailey.

"Recycle your homework," said Frank.

"And cans and bottles and stuff," said Leo.

"Turn garbage into dirt," said Rocky.

"Yes," said Mr. Todd. "That's called composting."

Judy raised her hand, knocking her note to the floor. "Plant trees!"

"Don't be litterbugs," said Jessica Finch.

"I wasn't littering," said Judy, picking up the note. She crossed out the Finch in Jessica's name and changed it to Jessica Fink. Sheesh. Sometimes Jessica Fink Finch gave her the jitterbugs.

"Great!" said Mr. Todd. "These are all good ideas. Look around you — at home, in school, on the playground — not just in Science class. How can we help the planet? How can we make the world around us a better place? We can each do our part. All it takes is one person to make a difference."

One person! If all it took was one person, then she, Judy Moody, could save the world!

She knew just where to start. With a banana peel.

On the way home from school that afternoon, Judy asked Rocky, "Hey, can you come over and eat some bananas?"

"Sure," said Rocky. "What for?"

"Compost," said Judy.

"I'll eat two!" said Rocky.

In Judy's kitchen, Judy and Rocky each ate one and a half bananas. They fed the fourth and last one to Mouse, Judy's cat. Then Judy tossed all four banana peels into a bucket.

"Why don't we make a sign for the bucket that says TURN GARBAGE INTO DIRT," said Rocky.

"Rare!" said Judy. "Tomorrow we can tell Mr. Todd how we started to heal the world."

"Double cool," said Rocky.

"Wait just a minute," said Judy. "Why didn't I think of it before? HEAL THE WORLD! That's it!"

"What's it?"

"My Band-Aid. For the Crazy Strips contest! You'll see." Judy ran upstairs and came back with markers and some paper. At the kitchen table, Rocky made a sign for the compost bucket while Judy drew a picture of Earth with a Band-Aid on it. She wrote HEAL THE WORLD under the globe in her best not-in-cursive letters. Then she drew banana peels all around the world.

Stink came into the kitchen. "What are you drawing?" he asked Judy.

"Banana peels," said Judy.

"For the Crazy Strip Contest," Rocky said.

"And you thought bats were weird?" said Stink. "Bats aren't half as crazy as banana peels."

He looked at the empty bowl on the table. "Hey! Who ate the last banana?"

"Mouse!" said Judy. Judy and Rocky fell on the floor laughing.

"No way," said Stink.

"Just look at her whiskers," said Judy.

Stink got down on the floor, face to face

with the cat. "Gross! Mouse has banana smoosh on her whiskers."

"Told you," said Judy.

"I'm telling Mom you ate all the bananas," said Stink. "And you fed one to Mouse."

"Tell her it's all in the name of science," said Judy. "You'll see. From now on there are going to be a few changes around here."

"We're making compost," said Rocky. "See?" He held up his sign.

"It takes like a hundred years to turn garbage into dirt," said Stink.

"Stink, *you're* going to be dirt. Unless you make like a tree and leaf us alone."

A Mr. Rubbish Mood

It was still dark out when Judy woke up early the next morning. She found her flashlight and notebook. Then she tiptoed downstairs to the kitchen and started to save the world.

She hoped she could save the world before breakfast. Judy wondered if other people making the world a better place had to do it quietly, and in the dark, so their parents would not wake up.

She, Judy Moody, was in a Mr. Rubbish mood. Mr. Rubbish was the Good Garbage Gremlin in Stink's comic book, who built his house out of French-fry cartons and pop bottles. He recycled everything, even lollipop sticks. And he never used anything from the rain forest.

Hmm . . . things that came from the rain forest. That would be a good place to start. Rubber came from the rain forest. And chocolate and spices and things like perfume. Even chewing gum.

Judy collected stuff from around the house and piled it on the kitchen table. Chocolate bars, brownie mix, vanilla ice cream. Her dad's coffee beans. The rubber toilet plunger. Gum from Stink's gumball machine. Her mom's lipstick from the bottom of her purse. She was so busy saving the rain forest that she didn't hear her family come into the kitchen.

"What in the world . . . ?" Mom said.

"Judy, why are you in the dark?" Dad asked, turning on the lights.

"Hey, my gumball machine!" Stink said.

Judy held out her arms to block the way. "We're not going to use this stuff anymore. It's all from the rain forest," she told them.

"Says who?" asked Stink.

"Says Mr. Rubbish. And Mr. Todd. They cut down way too many trees to grow coffee and give us makeup and chewing gum.

Mr. Todd says the earth is our home. We have to take action to save it. We don't need all this stuff."

"I need gum!" yelled Stink. "Give me back my gum!"

"Stink! Don't yell. Haven't you ever heard of noise pollution?"

"Is my coffee in there?" Dad asked, rubbing his hair.

"Judy? Is that ice cream? It's dripping all over the table!" Mom carried the leaky carton over to the sink.

"ZZZZ-ZZZZZ!" Judy made the sound of a chain saw cutting down trees.

"She's batty," Stink said.

Dad put the brownie mix back in the cupboard. Mom took the toilet plunger off the kitchen table and headed for the bathroom.

Time for Plan B. Project R. E. C. Y. C. L. E. She, Judy Moody, would show her family just how much they hurt the planet. Every time someone threw something away, she would write it down. She got her notebook and looked in the trash can. She wrote down:

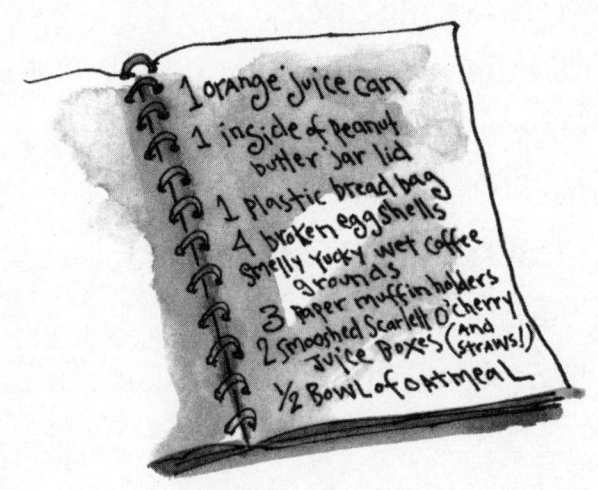

1 orange juice can
1 inside of peanut butter jar lid
1 plastic bread bag
4 broken eggshells
smelly yucky wet coffee grounds
3 paper muffin holders
2 smooshed Scarlett O'Cherry juice boxes (and straws!)
½ bowl of oatmeal

"Stink! You shouldn't throw gooey old oatmeal in the trash!" Judy said.

"Dad! Tell her to quit spying on me."

"I'm a Garbage Detective!" said Judy. "*Garbologist* to you. Mr. Todd says if you want to learn what to recycle, you have to get to know your garbage."

"Here," said Stink, sticking something wet and mushy under Judy's nose. "Get to know my apple core."

"Hardee-har-har," said Judy. "Hasn't anybody in this family ever heard of the Three R's?"

"The Three R's?" asked Dad.

"Re-use. Re-cycle."

"What's the third one?" asked Stink.

"Re-fuse to talk to little brothers until they quit throwing stuff away."

"Mom! I'm not going to stop throwing stuff away just because Judy's having a trash attack."

"Look at all this stuff we throw away!" Judy said. "Did you know that one person throws away more than eight pounds of garbage a day?"

"We recycle all our glass and cans," said Mom.

"And newspapers," Dad said.

"But what about this?" said Judy, picking a plastic bag out of the trash." This bread bag could be a purse! Or carry a library book."

"What's so great about eggshells?" asked Stink. "And smelly old ground-up coffee?"

"You can use them to feed plants. Or make compost." Just then, something in the trash caught her eye. A pile of Popsicle sticks? Judy pulled it out. "Hey! My Laura Ingalls Wilder log cabin I made in second grade!"

"It looks like a glue museum to me," said Stink.

"I'm sorry, Judy," Mom said. "I should have asked first, but we can't save everything, honey."

"Recycle it!" said Stink. "You could use it for kindling, to start a fire! Or break it down into toothpicks."

"Not funny, Stink."

"Judy, you're not even ready for school yet. Let's talk about this later," said Dad. "It's time to get dressed."

It was no use. Nobody listened to her. Judy trudged upstairs, feeling like a sloth without a tree.

"I won't wear lipstick today if it'll make you feel better," Mom called up the stairs.

"And I'll only drink half a cup of coffee," Dad said, but Judy could hardly hear him over the grinding of the rain forest coffee beans.

Her family sure knew how to ruin a perfectly good Mr. Rubbish mood. She put on her jeans and her Spotted Owl T-shirt. And to save water, she did not brush her teeth.

She clomped downstairs in a mad-at-your-whole-family mood.

"Here's your lunch," said Mom.

"Mom! It's in a paper bag!"

"What's wrong with that?" Stink asked.

"Don't you get it?" said Judy. "They cut down trees to make paper bags. Trees give shade. They help control global warming. We would die without trees. They make oxygen and help take dust and stuff out of the air."

"Dust!" said Mom. "Let's talk about cleaning your room if we're going to talk dust."

"Mo-om!" How was she supposed to do important things like save trees if she couldn't even save her *family* tree? That did it. Judy went straight to the garage and dug out her Sleeping Beauty lunch box from kindergarten.

"Are you really going to take that baby lunch box on the bus? Where the whole world can see?" asked Stink.

"I'm riding my bike today," said Judy. "To save energy."

"See you at school, then." Stink waved his *paper-bag* lunch at her. If only she could recycle her little brother.

"Go ahead. Be a tree hater," called Judy. "It's your funeral."

Making the world a better place sure was complicated.

Pigtoes, Pumas, and Pimplebacks

At school, Judy wiggled all during Math in the morning. She squirmed through Spelling. At last it was Science.

"Over half the world's plants and animals are found in rain forests," Mr. Todd said. "Which is why it's so important to protect the rain forest. The health of our whole planet depends on it. But did you know that there are endangered species right here in Virginia?"

Endangered species! Right here in Virginia! Judy leaned forward in her seat.

"If we want to take care of our planet, it helps to begin in our own backyard. That's why I'm asking each of you to adopt an endangered animal from Virginia this week. Tell us about the species, why it's disappearing, and what can be done to help."

Adopt an animal! She could help an endangered species. She, Judy Moody, could help save the entire state of Virginia!

Mr. Todd was shaking a coffee can. "Each slip of paper has the name of one endangered animal on it. When I call on you, come up and take one slip of paper from the can. Who wants to be first?"

All hands went up in the air.

"Rocky."

"Shenandoah salamander!" said Rocky, reading his slip of paper.

"Frank Pearl."

"Monkeyface mussel!"

Rare! Judy waved her hand in the air like a flag. Mr. Todd still did not call on her.

Brad got the bald eagle. Hailey got the puma. Randi got the leatherback sea turtle.

"Jessica Finch."

"Shiny pigtoe," said Jessica. "Yippee!"

Judy could not think of anybody else who would want to adopt a pig's toe. Only Jessica Finch. Jessica Finch liked everything about pigs. Even shiny pigs' toes.

While Mr. Todd called out more names, Judy turned around and said to Jessica,

"A shiny pigtoe is a pig with nail polish!" She cracked herself up.

"Judy Moody."

Judy turned around, her hand the only one still left in the air. "One left," said Mr. Todd. "C'mon up."

Finally! Judy unfolded the small slip of paper. "Northeast beach tiger beetle," she read.

Northeast beach tiger beetle! A northeast beach tiger beetle was not even an animal. It was a bug. An icketty cricketty old creepy crawly.

"If we don't like ours, can we trade?" Judy asked.

"I'd like everybody to stick with their choices," said Mr. Todd.

"What if we never even heard of it? What if we don't even know what it looks like?" said Judy.

"That's the fun of it," said Mr. Todd. "Find out. Go to the library and look at books and magazines. Or search the Web at the computer lab. And this Thursday, we'll be taking a class field trip to the museum, which should have information on all of your adopted animals."

"Big museum or little museum?" asked Frank.

"Little," said Mr. Todd. The class groaned.

The big museum meant the Smithsonian in Washington, D.C. Or the one with all the planes. The little museum meant the science museum down the street. It had toy trains, plastic dinosaurs, and one-hundred-year-old pictures of Virginia stuff.

"The best exhibit there is cobwebs," Rocky said.

☙ ☙ ☙

When Thursday came, Judy wore her tiger-striped pajama pants to school in honor of the tiger beetle. At the museum, Mr. Todd introduced the class to the museum lady. "This is Ms. Stickley, and she's going to tell us about endangered species in Virginia."

Ms. Stickley looked like a stick bug. Even her socks were brown.

"Call me Stephanie," said Ms. Stick Bug.

"Class," said Mr. Todd. "I expect you to give Stephanie your best third-grade listening ears." Frank pretended to take off his ears and hand them to her. Judy cracked up.

Ms. Stephanie Stick Bug took them on a tour of *Where the Wild Things Aren't*. She showed them a real live Shenandoah salamander, a Virginia fringed mountain snail that looked extremely sluggy, and a stuffed flying squirrel glued to a board.

"A flying squirrel! Is his name Rocky, like in *Rocky and Bullwinkle?*" asked Frank.

"Yes," said Ms. Stick Bug. "As a matter of fact it is."

"His name is Rocky, too!" said Frank, pointing at Rocky. "Hey, Rocky, you're a squirrel!"

"And you're Bullwinkle!" said Rocky. "You're a moose! Ha!"

Judy was dying to ask Ms. Stick Bug a

question. She raised her hand, holding it as straight as a shortnose sturgeon. At last, Stephanie called on her.

"Do you have any northeast beach tiger beetles?" asked Judy.

"No, I'm sorry we don't," said Stephanie. "Those *are* endangered in Virginia and that would be a good specimen for our collection."

What kind of endangered species museum did not have any northeast beach tiger beetles?

"Do you have any cave isopods?" asked Jessica Smartypants Finch.

"What's an ice-o-pod?" asked Rocky.

"An isopod is a crustacean like a sow bug," answered Stephanie. "Think of it like a pill bug, or a wood louse. You'll find those in Arachnid Hall."

"Ick! A louse is lice!" said Rocky.

Judy still couldn't see why they didn't have any northeast beach tiger beetles. After all, they had a bunch of creepy crustaceans, licey isopods, and pillbuggy pests.

Judy raised her hand again. She wanted to sound as smart as Jessica Finch.

"Excuse me," she said. "Do you have any two-toed sloths here? Tropical treehoppers? Nocturnal aye-ayes?"

"We don't have a rain forest exhibit," said Ms. Stick Bug. "But it's a great idea. Maybe someday."

The whole class got to touch an orange-foot pimpleback pearlymussel shell and hear a story about a Dismal Swamp shrew.

"Everything in this whole place is endangered," said Frank.

"My grade in Science is endangered, too," said Judy.

Beetle Emergency

The very next morning, Judy started her own search for a real live northeast beach tiger beetle. Before school, she grabbed a peanut butter jar from the recycling bin and ran out into the backyard. She tapped on tree bark. She crawled through itchy grass. She peered down into the dirt.

"Here, beetle, beetle," called Judy. "Don't be endangered."

She did not find one single beetle. All she found was an acorn hat, a slug, and a not-recycled candy wrapper.

"Judy!" called her Dad. "What are you doing out there in your pajamas?"

"Looking for a northeast beach tiger beetle," said Judy. "They're endangered. Mr. Todd says saving endangered species begins in your own backyard," said Judy.

"Not before breakfast in your pajamas," said Dad. "All the beetles are still sleeping."

At school that day, Judy searched for a picture of her beetle. And a few facts. She looked in the dictionary. She looked in the encyclopedia. She looked in bug books. She even looked on the computer. No luck.

Most of the beetles in the computer were the John Lennon and Paul McCartney kind of Beatles.

༺   ༺   ༺

The next day was Saturday. Frank Pearl called Judy. "Can I come over?"

"Not unless you bring a northeast beach tiger beetle with you."

"Okay," said Frank.

"You found one?" Judy asked. "For real?"

"Not a live one. But I found a picture of one. Do you have any stamps at your house?" asked Frank.

"What's stamps got to do with anything?"

"Just go see if you have any stamps. Stamps with bugs."

Judy put down the phone and ran to find some stamps in her parents' desk.

"Just boring old flags," she told Frank.

"Well, I have gazillions of stamps and—"

"How come you have so many stamps?"

"I collect them. I was pasting some in my album when I saw your beetle on one of the stamps."

"Bring it over right away," said Judy. "Tell your mom it's an emergency."

Half an hour later, Frank rang the doorbell. "Finally!" said Judy, pulling him into the living room.

Frank put his stamp album on the coffee table and opened it up. He turned to the Insects and Spiders page. "Look at all the beetles," said Frank. "That's a lady beetle—those are good luck. And there's a dung beetle, a Hercules beetle, and a spotted water beetle. Even an elderberry longhorn beetle."

"Which one is it?" Judy shrieked. Frank pointed to a beetle with a shiny green head and eyes like an alien. Printed below the beetle it said *Cicindela dorsalis dorsalis.*

"That's not a northeast beach tiger beetle," said Judy. "It's some kind of a Cinderella beetle."

"It's Latin," said Frank.

"Latin? Don't they have any beetles that speak English?"

"Read what it says underneath."

Northeast beach tiger beetle. Found along sandy beaches in the Chesapeake Bay areas of Virginia. Endangered by changes in habitat, human population, shoreline development, and erosion.

"My beetle's a beach bum! Thanks a million gazillion, Frank. Now I can work on my report. First I'll draw a picture for the cover."

"Want some help?" asked Frank.

"Sure," said Judy. "You can put the caps back on the markers."

Judy drew many-legged northeast beach tiger beetles all over the cover of her report. "Make sure they have biting mouth parts," said Frank. "And wings."

"Oh, yeah," said Judy.

"Can I help color them in?" asked Frank.

"Okay. Thanks," Judy said. "Did you already draw your cover for the monkey-face mussel?"

"Yeah," said Frank. "It's a seashell with bumps on it that look like a monkey's face. No lie. You can see eyes and ears and everything."

"I got to see that," said Judy. She printed the title of her report in all capitals. SAVE THE NORTHEAST BEACH TIGER BEETLE.

"Rare!" said Judy.

"Double cool," said Frank.

Just as she finished her cover, Stink came into the room and looked at Judy's drawing. "Why did you draw fat, flying footballs all over your report?"

Pond Scum

Judy worked on her report all weekend. In Science on Monday, the class presented its endangered species. Frank told the class how a monkeyface mussel got its name. Jessica Finch showed a shiny pigtoe shell that looked like a striped Hershey's Kiss. Judy bragged about the importance of the northeast beach tiger beetle.

"Tiger beetles recycle dead trees and eat tons of harmful insects, so don't step on

them. They are really fast and tricky, like tigers. Their rain forest cousin, the Hercules beetle, is six inches long! Tiger beetles make a loud buzzing sound, like this. *Bzzzzzzz!* The end."

When they were all finished, Mr. Todd said, "Good job! Thank you all for raising our awareness of these special creatures. Remember, if you find one of these animals in the wild, put it back. It's important not to remove creatures from their natural habitats."

Suddenly, Judy had an idea. An Einstein idea! It was time to call a secret club meeting. She passed a note to Frank: *Emergency meeting of the Toad Pee Club. Today! Pass this to Rocky.*

Jessica leaned forward, trying to see Judy's note. "I'll bet you can't spell the word *endangered*," hissed Jessica.

"Yes I can," said Judy. "G-O-N-E, gone."

Judy had ants in her pants all through Spelling.

Bzzzzzzz! At last the bell rang, like a sweet chorus of buzzing tiger beetles, and she, Judy Moody, was G-O-N-E, gone.

After school, Frank, Rocky, and Judy crawled inside the blue tent in Judy's backyard. While they waited for Stink, Judy whispered the plan to Frank and Rocky.

"I'll get rid of Stink," said Rocky.

"And I'll keep an eye on Toady," said Frank. Finally, Stink crawled inside the tent, carrying Toady, their mascot, in a yogurt container.

"Where are we gonna put Toady?" asked Stink.

"Over here in the corner by me," said Frank. "I'll guard him."

"And don't pick him up with your bare hands, Stink, or he'll get you. *If* you know what I mean," Judy warned him.

"Hey, did you know if you change two letters around in *T-o-a-d-y* you get *t-o-d-a-y*?" asked Stink.

"That's nice, Stink," said Judy. "Did you know if you add three letters to Stink you get Stinkbug?"

Stink ignored her. "It's squishy in here," he complained.

"Try making yourself a little smaller, Stink. People take up way too much room on the planet. That's why we have so many problems."

"Oh brother," said Stink. "Why are we here anyway?"

"No reason," said Rocky. He kicked Frank's shoe and Frank nudged Judy and all three cracked up.

"Let's brainstorm," said Frank. "You know, think up stuff we can do in our club.

Even though it's really hot and crowded in here."

"I'm too squished. It's too hot in here to brainstorm," said Stink.

"It's global warming," said Judy. "Right here in Virginia."

Stink panted like a dog. "Stink. Don't breathe so much. You'll ruin the ozone," said Judy. "There's already a hole over Antarctica!"

"You're in the ozone," said Stink. He crawled out of the tent.

"Perfect!" said Judy. Judy, Rocky, and Frank double high-fived each other.

"And he forgot to take Toady!" said Rocky.

"T-o-d-a-y is your lucky day, T-o-a-d-y.

Today is the day we save the world, starting with you," Judy said.

Frank picked up Toady. Toady blinked. "He doesn't look endangered!"

"No, but your hand is endangered," said Judy. "Better put him back."

"I kind of hate to see him go," said Frank.

"But Mr. Todd said! Remember? If you catch a creature in the wild you have to put it back. Toadnapping is the same thing as hurting the planet," Judy explained.

"Just think how happy he'll be," said Rocky.

They carried Toady down to the stream behind Judy's house. "I'll miss you, Toady," Judy said. "But the time has come for you to join your toady friends and do your

toady things. Go make this planet a better place." On the count of three, Judy, Rocky, and Frank gently tipped the yogurt container on its side and let Toady go.

"Goodbye, Toadster!" said Rocky.

"Watch out for acid rain!" said Frank. Toady blinked once, then *bloomp!* He plopped into the water. In one, two, three bubbles, Toady was gone.

"Nice sendoff," said Frank.

"It's for a good cause," said Rocky.

"Toadly awesome!" said Judy.

Rocky and Frank went home. She, Judy Moody, was on her way to making the world a better place. The Toad Pee Club had taken one small step for toadkind and one giant leapfrog for humankind.

It took Stink one hour and twenty-eight minutes to notice that Toady was missing. Endangered, as in G-O-N-E, gone.

"Toady's gone?" asked Stink. "Oh, no! What if he got swallowed by a snake? Or gobbled by a giant hawk? It's all my fault for leaving him in the tent. Why didn't you *do* something?"

"I did," said Judy, and she broke the good news about letting Toady go to make the planet a better place.

If Stink were a poison dart frog, he would have spit poison at Judy. If Stink were a volcano, he would have spewed lava.

"It's not fair!" Stink moaned. "Toady was my pet!"

"Toady belonged to all the members of the Toad Pee Club."

"But I took care of him mostly," said Stink. "How can letting him go make the world a better place? It makes it a worse place if you ask me."

"Stink, you'd be pond scum if you kept Toady locked up in that aquarium," said

Judy. "That aquarium is like being in jail."

"*You're* gonna be in jail as soon as I tell Mom and Dad."

"Look at it this way. Toady gets to be free and now there will be even more toads. Don't you get it?"

"I get that you stole my toad."

Sometimes Stink could be as stubborn as a hard-headed hornbill.

"Now we don't even have a mascot for our club," said Stink.

Judy grabbed Mouse. "Mouse could be our new mascot!"

"The Mouse Pee Club? I don't think so," said Stink. "See? If it wasn't for Toady, there wouldn't even be a Toad Pee Club."

"There will be other toads to pee on us, Stink. I promise."

"I'm still telling," said Stink.

Luna Two

The next day, Judy came home from school and climbed a tree.

She, Judy Moody, was in Trouble with a capital T. Why was her whole family mad at her for letting a toad go free? She was just doing her part to save the world.

Stink saw her up in the tree. "Hey. No fair! Mom and Dad said you had to go straight to your room!"

"This *is* my room," Judy said. "I'm going to live up here now. Like Julia Butterfly Hill."

"Who?"

"The girl who lived in a tree for two years. Mr. Todd told us. They were going to cut down some ancient redwoods in California. So Julia Butterfly Hill climbed one of the trees and stayed there. They couldn't cut down a tree with a person in it. She even named the tree Luna."

"You can't just live in a tree, Judy," said Stink.

"Judy Monarch Moody to you."

"Oh, brother," said Stink.

"If I live in this tree, newspapers will come. And TV people. Everybody will learn how important trees are. I'll call my tree Luna Two."

"How about luna-tic," said Stink.

"Hardee-har-har," said Judy. "Stink, you will have to be the gofer."

"Gopher? A gopher sounds like a rat."

"An *important* rat," said Judy. "Go get me my walkie-talkies. It will be like Julia Butterfly Hill's solar-powered cell phone. That's how I'll talk to people."

Stink came back with the walkie-talkies. Judy climbed down to a lower branch and Stink stood on a milk crate to pass them up to her.

"Now get me a flashlight. It's going to get dark up here."

Stink went and got the flashlight.

"Now can you get me a glass of water?" asked Judy.

"Water? What's the water for?" asked Stink.

"I'm thirsty!"

"Forget it," said Stink.

"I'll pay you fifty cents."

"How long are you going to be up there?" Stink asked, thinking of all the money he could make.

"Julia Butterfly Hill was in her tree for seven hundred and thirty-eight days. Sooner or later, Stink, you're going to have to get me some water. And lentils. Julia Butterfly Hill ate lentils."

"Lentils! You never ate a lentil in your life!" Stink said. He got a bottle of water.

"You owe me fifty cents," said Stink. "We're all out of lentils. I forgot I used them to make my Empire State Building in Social Studies."

"I guess I'll learn to like lima beans," said Judy. "Ick."

"Rocky's on his way over," said Stink. "He called and I told him you live in a tree now. I told him you are going to be in big trouble when Mom and Dad find out you didn't go straight to your room."

"This *is* my room."

"Then can I have your room inside the house?"

🌀   🌀   🌀

Rocky raced around the corner into the backyard. "What's up, Judy? Besides you, I mean?" He cracked himself up.

Judy didn't laugh. Judy didn't say a word.

"You have to call her Judy Monarch Moody," said Stink.

"Oh, I get it," said Rocky. "Like that girl who lived in the tree. What are you going to do if it rains?"

"I'll stay under the leaves," said Judy.

"What about when it gets dark?" asked Rocky.

"I have a flashlight," said Judy.

"See what I mean?" said Stink. "First she went crazy over some trash. Then it was a weird beetle. She's driving *me* up a tree!"

"Oh, no! Not you too?" Rocky and Stink fell on the ground laughing.

"How are we going to get her to come down?" Stink asked Rocky.

"Mr. Todd said the tree cutters tried playing loud music and shining bright lights at Julia Butterfly Hill all night to make her come down," said Rocky.

"Time for Operation Boom Box," said Stink.

They blasted loud music to annoy Judy into coming down. She just put her hands over her ears and hummed, "O Beautiful for Spacious Skies."

"What else did they try on Julia?" asked Stink.

"Lawsuits," said Rocky.

"I'll sue you if you don't come down!" yelled Stink.

"For what?" asked Judy.

"For staying up in a tree and getting out of your punishment or something."

"Or something," said Judy.

"Let's try shaking the tree," said Rocky. They put their hands around the tree and shook, but the tree did not budge one leaf.

"Tree bark is worse than bug bites," Stink said, showing his scraped-up arm. "Hey, Judy, I need a doctor. For real. Go get your doctor kit."

"Nice try," said Judy Monarch Moody.

Just then, Mouse came outside and bolted up the tree.

"Thanks for the company," called Judy. "Now I won't get lonely up here."

"Great," said Stink. "Now Mouse won't come down either. And we'll have to call her Mouse Swallowtail Moody or something."

"I have to stay up here," said Judy. "For the sake of all trees. And owls and flying squirrels and all the things that need trees. Even people. And toads."

"Let's just leave her up there," said Stink. "Who cares if she falls? Who cares if she gets in big trouble?"

"Even Judy Monarch Moody can't stay up there forever. You have to go to school," called Rocky.

"Julia Butterfly Hill got a Ph.D. from a college while she was up in the tree," Judy called back.

"Maybe if we ignore her she'll come down," said Rocky.

"Operation Ignore Judy," said Stink.

Stink and Rocky went inside. Mouse leaped down from a branch and followed them. "Traitor!" Judy yelled after her cat.

Living in a tree was a little lonely. Judy wondered if Julia Butterfly Hill got lonely, too. Seven hundred and thirty-eight days was a long time. Judy had hardly lasted seven hundred and thirty-eight seconds.

A few minutes later, Stink and Rocky ran

back outside. Stink waved an envelope in the air. "Hey you, up there," said Stink. "Judy Monarch Moody."

"What now?" asked Judy.

"You got a letter from the Crazy Strips Contest!" Rocky yelled up at her.

"Really?" said Judy, looking down from her perch. "Open it and read it to me."

"No way," said Stink. "You have to come down and find out for yourself."

"I'm not going to fall for that trick, Stink," said Judy.

"I'll read it," said Stink. He opened the envelope. He unfolded the letter. *"Dear Judy Moody,"* read Stink. "I guess they don't know your middle name is Monarch."

"Just read it!" said Judy.

"Congratulations! You are a winner of the Crazy Strips Design Your Own Bandage Contest."

Judy could not believe her ears! She dropped down from her branch in Luna

Two like a leopard to its prey. "Let me see that!" Out loud, she read,

Stink and Rocky cracked up as bad as a Brazil nut.

"STINK!" Judy wailed. "You tricked me. This is not from the Crazy Strips Company. You got me out of my tree because the dentist missed my smile?"

"It worked," said Stink.

"Take a good look at this smile," said

Judy, baring her teeth, Siberian tiger–style.

"Does this mean I can't have your room?" asked Stink.

"ROAR!" said Judy.

Batty for Band-Aids

When Judy, Stink, and Rocky got off the bus after school the next day, Stink called, "Race you to the mailbox!" But Judy did not run after Stink. She stayed right where she was so she could watch Rocky do his new disappearing-bubble-gum trick. That's when they heard Stink yell from across the street, "The Crazy Strips Contest! Judy, you won!" He waved an envelope in the air.

"Stink, you lie like a rug!" Judy said. "I'm not falling for that trick again."

"It says CONTEST WINNER. Right here in fat red letters. See?"

"If this is a trick, *you're* up a tree," Judy said, crossing the street.

"Maybe it's not a trick this time," said Rocky, walking beside her. "What did she win?"

"Rollerblades!" said Stink.

"Rollerblades do not fit in an envelope, Stink."

"Maybe you're a runner-up, then," said Stink. "Maybe you won sunglasses."

"Sunglasses don't fit in an envelope either. Give it." Judy grabbed the envelope and tore it open.

"Certificate?" yelled Judy. "That's all I get for HEAL THE WORLD? One crummy certificate? A certificate is not even close to Rollerblades. A certificate will not decorate the ankles of millions."

"An Honorable Mention certificate is like winning second place," said Rocky.

Judy covered up her ears. "Don't even *mention* the word certificate again."

"At least you got *something*," Stink said.

"Yeah," Rocky said. "Stink didn't even get a certificate."

That cheered Judy up a little. "Well, at least I get to hang something in the Moody Hall of Fame on the fridge."

Just then, Stink dropped the mail. Catalogs and envelopes blew every which way. "Help!" yelled Stink. A letter flew out from inside a catalog and landed on the driveway.

"Wait!" called Stink, picking up the letter. "I got one too!"

"Let's see if you still think certificates are so great," said Judy.

Stink took his time opening the envelope.

"Stink, I'll be in fourth grade by the time you get that open. Hurry up. Read it!"

Stink read the letter.

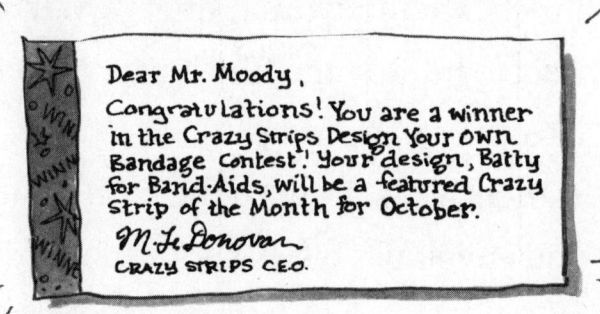

"Crazy Strip of the Month!" said Stink, jumping up and down and waving the letter in the air. "I got Crazy Strip of the Month!"

"Let me see that." Judy read the letter with her own eyes. How could this happen? Her very own stinky little brother won Crazy Strip of the Month!

"What's wrong with these people?" cried Judy, shaking the letter. Did they have bats in their belfries? Band-Aids for brains? "Don't they know bats have beady little eyes and squished-up noses like pigs? Don't they know bats look like vampires?"

"At least they don't look like flying footballs," said Stink.

"Don't they even care about healing the world?" Judy said.

"Big-eared bats are endangered," said Stink. "Putting them on a Crazy Strip is like healing the world."

"ROAR!" said Judy. Big-eared bats were going to decorate the ankles of millions. Meanwhile, the entire state of Virginia would be stepping on northeast beach tiger beetles and not even knowing it.

"Hey! What about your Rollerblades?" asked Rocky.

"It says here I won a pair of Crazy Strips sunglasses," said Stink.

"That must be your prize," said Rocky, pointing to a big box on the porch. Stink and Rocky ran over, with Judy right behind them.

"It's from the Crazy Strips company!" said Stink. "My sunglasses!"

"They must be sunglasses for a rhino," said Judy.

"Maybe they messed up and sent you Rollerblades by mistake," said Rocky.

"I hope they're black with a red racing stripe and a silver—"

"Stink! Just open the box!" said Judy.

Stink ripped into the box. It was not Rollerblades. It was not sunglasses for a rhino. It was Crazy Strips. Tons of Crazy Strips. Gazillions of Crazy Strips. A lifetime supply! At least ten boxes!

"Rare!" whispered Judy.

"Wow-wee!" said Rocky. "I've never seen so many Crazy Strips."

"I have," said Stink, pointing to Judy, Queen of the Crazy Strips. "But these are M-I-N-E, mine."

"You drew this?" asked Rocky, looking at Stink's design. "Double cool."

"Wow, your very own original Crazy Strip," said Judy. She couldn't help feeling like a green bean. *Green* with envy.

"Hey! Here's my sunglasses," said Stink, digging down to the bottom of the box. They were shaped like a Band-Aid. He put them on and looked at the sun. "They really work!" said Stink.

"Luck-y!" said Judy. "Those will protect you from that giant hole in the ozone over Antarctica."

Stink had his own Crazy Strip! Her very own batty little brother was now as famous as Josephine Dickson, Inventor of the Adhesive Bandage. If it weren't for that giant hole in the sky, she, Judy Moody, would move to Antarctica.

"Do you think they have bats in Antarctica?" Judy asked.

"Frozen bats," said Stink.

Ow-oooo! Judy tipped her head toward the ozone and let out one long howler-monkey howl.

Project P.E.N.C.I.L.

The next morning, and the next one after that, Judy woke up feeling like a sloth moth. She could hardly make herself get out of bed.

Saving the world was not going so well. She hadn't done anything *really* important. Like heal the world with her own Crazy Strip. So far, she had only saved four banana peels, a lunch bag, and a toad.

On Friday morning, Judy ate her no-garbage breakfast in silence. She packed her no-garbage lunch by herself. She didn't say a word when Stink stuck Crazy Strips all over his arms, elbows, knees, and chin.

"These Crazy Strips itch," said Stink, peeling off the one on his elbow. Judy couldn't stand it one more minute.

"If those were my Crazy Strips," said Judy, "I'd be happy to itch. I would not scratch once. And I would never not ever peel it off. Not even in the bathtub."

༄ ༄ ༄

In school, Judy did not raise her hand once. She did not pass a note to Frank. She did nothing but chew her Grouchy pencil all through Spelling.

She, Judy Moody, was in a pencil-snapping mood.

When it was time for Science, Mr. Todd took off his watch and said, "I want everybody to sit still for sixty seconds. I'll time you." When the minute was up, Mr. Todd said, "In that minute, one hundred acres of trees in the rain forest were just destroyed.

That's seventy football fields."

"No way!" went through the class.

"We all depend on the rain forest," said Mr. Todd. "For things we eat and wear and use every single day. Think about it. Even your wooden pencil and rubber eraser could be from the rain forest. Ninety-eight percent of the cedar wood used for pencils comes from rain forest trees."

Judy stopped chewing on her Grouchy pencil. She stared at it. The grouchy face looked even grouchier. This pencil used to be a tree. A rain forest tree!

She, Judy Moody, would never, ever use a pencil again.

Not even a Grouchy pencil.

"If we help save the rain forest, we help save the planet," said Mr. Todd.

Suddenly, Judy had a plan. A perfect Save-the-World plan. All she had to do was skip recess.

When all the kids hurried outside to the playground, Judy sneaked back to the classroom. This was her big chance. Inside each desk was a pencil holder. Judy raced around the room and took the pencils from each desk. Then she hid them inside the flower vase.

As soon as recess was over, it was time for Math. "Take out your workbooks," said Mr. Todd. "Let's get those pencils working."

Uh-oh! Judy thought.

"Hey, my pencil's gone!"

"Mine too!"

"Mine was right here!"

"Mr. Todd! Mr. Todd! Somebody stole our pencils!" The whole class was in an uproar.

"Okay, is somebody playing a joke?" asked Mr. Todd. Nobody answered. "Do any of you know anything about the missing pencils?"

Judy kept her head down and pretended to work out math problems. Brad looked at Judy. She was the only one NOT complaining about her missing pencil. And she was doing math problems with a *p-e-n*.

"Pencil thief!" Brad yelled, pointing at her. "Judy Moody stole our pencils!"

Judy felt the eyes of twenty-one third-grade pencil lovers turn to glare at her.

"Judy?" Mr. Todd came over to her desk. "What do you know about these missing pencils?"

"Okay, I took them," Judy confessed. "Because I think we should stop using pencils."

"Stop using pencils? That's nuts!" Brad said.

"To help save the rain forest," said Judy.

"Hmm. Class, what do you think?" asked Mr. Todd.

"We just want our pencils back," said Leo.

Judy could not believe these third-grade pencil freaks! Were they in the ozone? Didn't they care that seventy football fields of trees a minute were being cut down? She wished they would all move to PENCILvania.

"I think we *should* save the rain forest," said Frank.

"Me too," said Hailey.

"Me three," Rocky said.

"Yeah, but we can't just give up pencils forever," said Randi. "We have to write stuff, and erase. Like in Math. How can we save the world without math?"

"Maybe we don't have to use so many," said Jessica Finch. "One pencil can draw a line thirty-five miles long. We could all promise to use the same pencil until fifth grade."

How did Jessica Fink Finch know so much

about pencils? Maybe she wasn't such a fink after all.

"How many pencils can you get from a tree?" Judy asked.

"None," said Brad. "Pencils don't grow on trees."

"Hardee-har-har," said Judy. "I mean it. You can get a lot of pencils from one tree. For real."

"One tree can make 172,000 pencils!" said Jessica Finch. "I read it in my *Ranger Rick* magazine."

"Wow! One tree could make all the pencils in our school."

"All the pencils in Virginia!"

"We could plant a tree in the rain forest, then," said Judy. "You know, for the Virginia Dare School. To make up for all the pencils we use."

"Kids all over the world raise money to protect rain forests," Jessica told the class. "It only costs a dollar to have one tree planted in the Children's Rain Forest in Costa Rica."

"If it only costs a dollar," Judy said, "then we could send money for them to plant trees, and our class can adopt them."

"Wow!" everybody said. "Let's do it."

"Class? Any ideas about how to raise some money?" Mr. Todd asked.

"How about a car wash?" said Lucy.

"We could sell stuff," said Adam. "Like cookies!"

"My sister put on a play in fifth grade and made money to help save the whales," said Jessica. "She even won a Giraffe Award for it."

A Giraffe Award! For somebody who sticks their neck out for a good cause. Judy could hardly wait till fifth grade!

"Maybe we could put on a magic show," said Rocky.

"Or we could collect a bunch of stuff to recycle," said Frank, "and get money for it. The Recycle Center gives five cents each for pop bottles and milk jugs."

"Rare!" said Judy.

"Double cool!" said Rocky.

"A bottle drive sounds like a fine idea," said Mr. Todd. "We could raise money while recycling at the same time. What do you say, class? Do you think we could collect enough bottles?"

"Yeah!" everybody yelled.

It was settled. The Virginia Dare School, Class 3T, was going into the bottle business. Starting with their very own cafeteria.

৯ ৯ ৯

The third-graders spent the afternoon rounding up milk jugs from all over the school. They piled up plastic bottles from the kindergarten classes, and from the teachers' lunchroom. They even rescued some from the trash.

Class 3T worked as hard as an army of leaf-cutter ants. "That was cool how you got us out of Math," whispered Frank.

"This is more fun than when you put my arm in a cast," said Jessica.

"We still need a ton more bottles if we're going to save the rain forest," said Rocky.

"Rocky's right," said Mr. Todd. "Let's go home and see how many bottles we can collect over the weekend. Ask your family and neighbors. Tell your friends."

Judy Moody felt as sharp as a pencil point. They were just a few days and a few hundred bottles away from saving the rain forest.

She was in a Judy-Moody-best-mood-ever. At last she was on her way to saving the world. And the best part was she no longer had to do it all by herself. Class 3T would save the world together. Like an ecosystem!

She, Judy Monarch Moody, knew just how a butterfly felt coming out of the chrysalis. Light as a feather.

Batty for Bottles

"Let's go on a bottle hunt," said Rocky. "After school."

"I sure hope bottles are easier to find than northeast beach tiger beetles," Judy said.

They raided Rocky's garage first and found two milk crates full of bottles that had not been recycled. "Rare!" said Judy. "Twenty-seven bottles!"

"But they're all smooshed. I forgot my mom stomps them."

"That's okay," said Judy. "They're ABC bottles. Already Been Crushed!"

At Judy's, her mother let her have the stash of milk jugs she was saving to make bird feeders. Dad didn't have any bottles, so he gave Rocky and Judy one dollar bill each to plant a tree.

"Thanks, Mr. Moody!" said Rocky.

Judy kissed George Washington right on his presidential nose.

"Does this mean I can wear lipstick again?" asked Mom.

"And I can drink coffee?" said Dad.

"Yes. But not too much," laughed Judy.

"No fair," said Stink. "I'd plant a tree, too, if I could have a dollar or something."

"Or something," said Judy.

🌀 🌀 🌀

All the next week, Class 3T piled up a mountain of bottles in the multipurpose room. Bags of bottles, boxes of bottles, bins full of bottles. "Great teamwork, class," said Mr. Todd. "Did you know we throw away two and a half million plastic bottles every hour in this country? In three months, we throw away enough bottles to circle the globe."

"Look out!" said Rocky. "Bottles are taking over the earth!"

"People should recycle them," said

Jessica Finch. "My dad has a jacket made out of recycled plastic bottles. My socks are made out of bottles, too."

"No way," said Judy. She turned around to take a look at the plastic-bottle socks. They looked regular. They did not look plastic at all.

"It's true," said Mr. Todd. "All that plastic can be recycled to make toys and coat hangers and picture frames. Even recycling bins!"

"How many bottles do you think we have so far?" asked Jessica.

"Let's pile them up all together to see how high they go," said Brad.

Class 3T spent their Math class piling up bottles and more bottles.

"We should call it Bottle Mountain," said Rocky.

"Double cool," said Frank. "It looks like a giant igloo."

When they had added every last bottle, Mr. Todd said, "Tomorrow's the big day. Tomorrow we'll find out the grand total number of bottles we have. Our principal, Ms. Tuxedo, will make an announcement to tell the school how much money we've raised. Now let's hurry back to class so nobody misses the bus."

"Tomorrow!" said Judy. "That's twenty-four more hours!" She couldn't wait to find out how many trees would be planted in the rain forest for the Virginia Dare School.

The Winking Disease

When Judy and Rocky stepped off the bus on Friday morning, Ms. Tuxedo was standing outside the school doors. "How's it going, you two?"

"Pretty good, I guess," said Judy.

"Today we find out how many trees we're going to plant," said Rocky.

"That's right," the principal said. "You both have a good day." And she winked. Judy looked at Rocky. Rocky looked at Judy.

In Judy Moody's entire third-grade life, she was sure she had never seen the principal wink at anybody.

Judy and Rocky hurried to the multipurpose room before class to look at the mountain of bottles again, but the doors were locked. When they got to 3T, Mr. Todd was standing in the doorway. "Isn't it a lovely Friday?" he said. Then he winked. In Judy Moody's entire third-grade life, she had never heard Mr. Todd say the word *lovely*. And for sure and absolute positive, she had never seen him wink.

"Something's up," she told Rocky.

Judy sat down next to Frank. "Know what? Something's funny. All the teachers have a winking disease today."

"A winking disease?"

"Yeah, you know, when they wink at you and say nice things."

While Judy waited for the day to begin, she looked around the room at all the kids in her ecosystem. Not one third-grader was absent. And every single person in Class 3T had pitched in and collected bottles.

"Class," said Mr. Todd, blinking the lights to get their attention. "Announcements. Listen up."

Judy Moody squirmed all through morning announcements. A Mexican jumping bean could have done a better job of sitting still.

"And now," came Ms. Tuxedo's voice over the PA system, "the moment you've been waiting for . . ." Judy Moody sat up super straight and used her best third-grade listening ears.

"As you know, Mr. Todd's room, Class 3T, has been collecting bottles this week to raise money for the rain forest. This money will go, on behalf of the Virginia Dare School, to plant trees in the Children's Rain Forest in Costa Rica. Thanks to Class 3T, the Virginia Dare School has collected 1,961 bottles. That means we will be planting ninety-eight trees to help save the rain forest."

Ninety-eight! Suddenly, Judy remembered the dollars from her dad. Two more dollars meant two more trees. One hundred trees! Class 3T went wild, jumping up and down, clapping and whooping and hooting like owls.

"We'd like to show our appreciation to our third graders in a special assembly today at 2:30. This will provide the whole school with a chance to give them a big hand and show them how proud we are of their hard work and their efforts for such a good cause."

"Lunch today is Sloppy Joes," Ms. Tuxedo continued. "Tickets go on sale Monday for the school fair. And will Judy Moody please report to the front office?"

"Uh-oh. Judy's in trouble," Jessica Finch said.

"Nobody's in trouble," said Mr. Todd. "Judy's going to represent our class at the assembly today. After all, she got us thinking about our pencils, and before we knew it, we were planting trees in the rain forest. Judy, go ahead down to the office and find out what Ms. Tuxedo would like you to do."

Judy walked as fast as she could without running down the great green halls of the Virginia Dare School to the front office. The third-grade papier-mâché masks outside the classroom seemed to wink at her. The second-grade self-portraits grinned. And the first-grade sunflowers on the wall stood up prouder.

Ms. Tuxedo took Judy into the multi-purpose room. The principal showed Judy where to sit in the front row and told her when to come up on stage.

"When I call you up on stage, I'll hand you something for your class. You accept it, then walk across the stage and rejoin your class."

"Is it a certificate?" asked Judy.

"It's a surprise! It'll be fun. You'll see," said the principal. And she winked. So *this* is what all the winking is about, Judy thought.

At 2:25, Mr. Todd's class hurried to the multipurpose room. Judy took her seat in the front row.

The room was dark. The curtains went up. A single spotlight shone on Ms. Tuxedo. Everybody clapped.

"Today, boys and girls, we are here to show how proud we are of Class 3T. They showed excellent teamwork on a project raising money to plant trees in the Children's Rain Forest in Costa Rica. Because of them, one hundred trees will be planted for the Virginia Dare School. Margaret Mead says, 'Never doubt that a small group of concerned people can change the world.' Our special thanks to 3T for helping to change the world!"

Everybody cheered and clapped some more.

"Ranger Piner is here as our special guest from the County Parks Department. They have donated a cedar tree, like the ones in the rain forest, to the Virginia Dare School.

Right after the assembly, Ranger Piner will help Mr. Todd's class plant the tree in front of our school.

"To show our appreciation, I have here, for every member of the class, a T-shirt and a gift certificate for one free Rain Forest Mist ice-cream cone from Screamin' Mimi's." Ms. Tuxedo waved an envelope in the air, and held up one of the T-shirts. It said TURN PLASTIC INTO TREES under a picture of a tree made out of bottles.

Judy's class jumped up and down and hooted some more. A T-shirt with words! And the kind of certificate that got you a free ice cream! Saving the world was even better than Judy thought.

"There's one person who proved to be a good friend to the whole planet and I'd like her to come up on stage — Judy Moody!"

Judy looked back at Mr. Todd. He motioned for her to go up on stage.

Judy Moody stood in the bright beam of light and tried not to squint. She looked out at all her classmates from 3T who had helped plant trees to save the rain forest. They waved their hands in the air and gave a howler-monkey hoot.

Ms. Tuxedo continued. "Usually this award goes to one fifth-grade student, but today, I think the whole third-grade class is deserving."

Award! Judy stood up straighter.

"Class 3T has made a contribution that will help not only our community, but the larger community — our planet, our world. Judy Moody and Class 3T, let me present — the award for somebody who really sticks their neck out — the Giraffe Award!"

The Giraffe! Judy could not believe her ears. Even her best third-grade listening ears. Everybody wanted to be a Giraffe when they got to fifth grade. She, Judy Moody, was a Giraffe in third grade!

Ms. Tuxedo handed her a gold trophy of a giraffe. "Let's give a big hand for 3T!"

Then, all of the third-grade Giraffes came up on stage to join hands and get their pictures taken in their new bottle-tree T-shirts. Cameras snapped and bulbs flashed. One of the cameras was Dad!

Dad reached up to give Judy a hug. "I brought the car," said Dad. "Thought I'd help take bottles to the Recycling Center after school."

"Rare!" said Judy.

"We're proud of you, kiddo," said Dad. "All of you."

Judy smiled. Not a Siberian-tiger smile. A real smile. The kind the dentist would really miss seeing.

Class 3T had joined together to make a difference. One hundred brand-new trees would be planted, like a Band-Aid for the rain forest. And she, Judy Moody, had played a small part in saving the world.

Judy stood in the center of the 3T ecosystem. She held the trophy high, and stretched her neck tall as a true Giraffe.

Megan McDonald

is the award-winning author of the Judy Moody series. She says that most of Judy's stories "grew out of anecdotes about growing up with my four sisters." She confesses, "I *am* Judy Moody. Same-same! In my family of sisters, we're famous for exaggeration. Judy Moody is me . . . exaggerated." Megan McDonald lives with her husband in northern California.

Peter H. Reynolds

says he felt an immediate connection to Judy Moody because, "having a daughter, I have witnessed firsthand the adventures of a very independent-minded girl." Peter H. Reynolds lives in Massachusetts, just down the street from his twin brother.

Praise for Judy Moody Saves the World!

A Book Sense 76 Selection

An American Library Association Amelia Bloomer Project Selection

An International Reading Association Children's Choice

A Chicago Public Library Best Book

An Oppenheim Toy Portfolio Gold Award Winner

"This charming read features characteristically snappy, humorous prose; expressive, witty black-and-white illustrations; and some great ideas for classroom or home projects." — *Booklist*

"Judy's growing corps of fans will crow 'Rare!' right along with her." — *Kirkus Reviews*

"*Judy Moody Saves the World!* is cleverly written, and its heroine is an appealing and very real third grader."
— *The Five Owls*

Be sure to read Judy's next adventure!

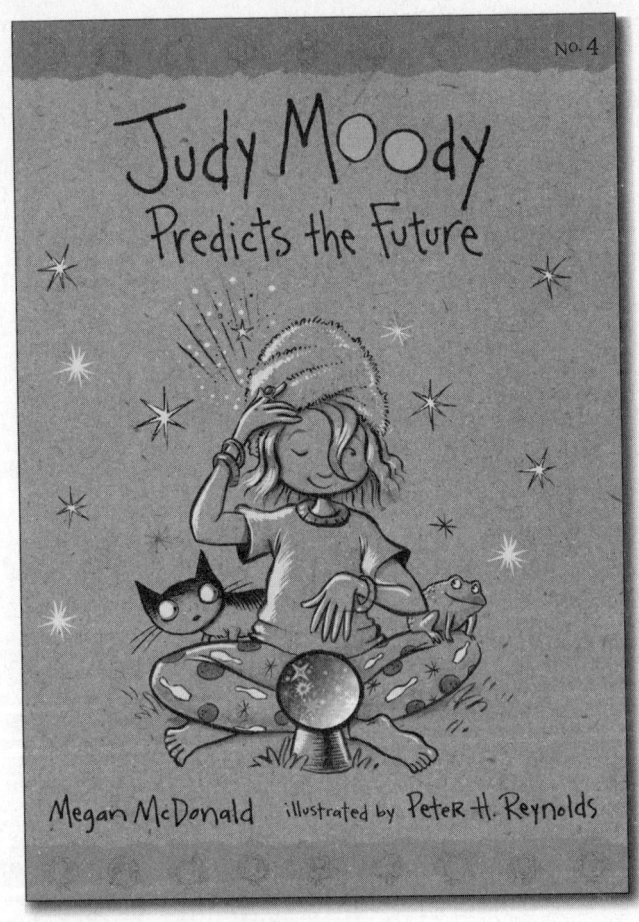

JUDY MOODY HAS HER OWN WEBSITE!
Visit it at **www.judymoody.com**

And check out Stink's adventures!

Experience all of Judy Moody's moods!